MW00946788

Alitji in Dreamland

Alitjinya Ngura Tjukurmankuntjala

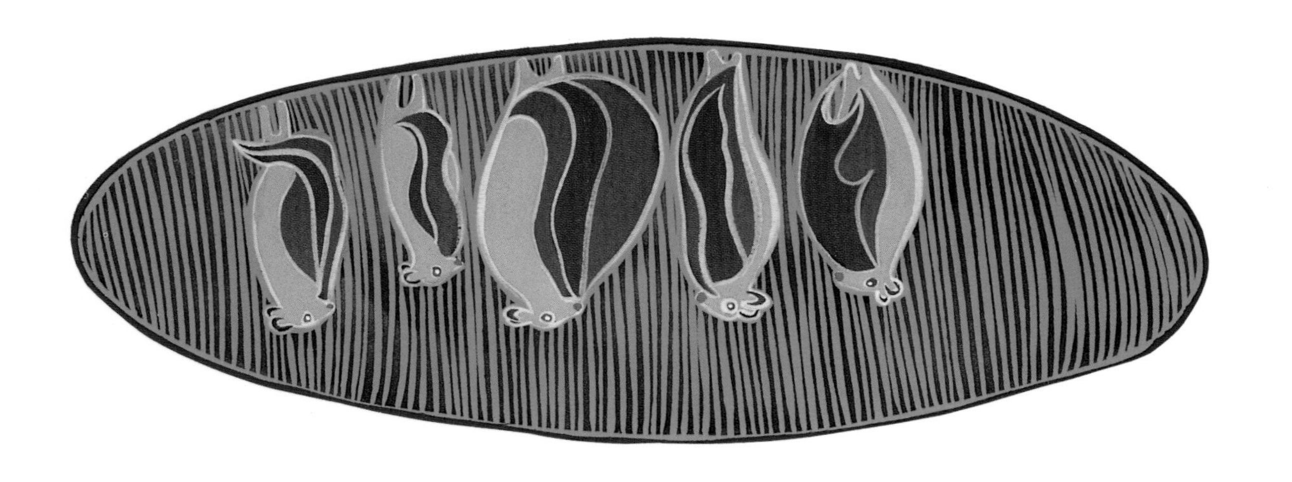

Alitji in Dreamland
Alitjinya Ngura Tjukurmankuntjala

An Aboriginal version of
LEWIS CARROLL'S ALICE'S ADVENTURES IN WONDERLAND

Adapted and translated by
NANCY SHEPPARD

Illustrated by
DONNA LESLIE

Notes by
BARBARA KER WILSON

TEN SPEED PRESS
Berkeley, California

ALITJI IN DREAMLAND/ALITJINYA NGURA TJUKURMANKUNTJALA

First published in Australia in 1975 by
The Department of Adult Education
The University of Adelaide
North Terrace, Adelaide
South Australia 5000

This edition first published in 1992 by
Simon & Schuster Australia
20 Barcoo Street, East Roseville NSW 2069

A Paramount Communications Company
Sydney New York London Toronto Tokyo Singapore

ISBN 0-89815-478-2

Ten Speed Press
Box 7123
Berkeley, CA 94707

Designed by Diana Kureen

Typeset in Korinna and Novarese by Savage Type Pty Ltd, Brisbane.

Printed in Hong Kong by South China Printing Co. Ltd.

1 2 3 4 5 – 96 95 94 93 92

Kampa

Contents

Pitingka Tjarpantja

Alitjinya karungka rawa nyinara pakuringangi. Kangkurura pula nyinara milpatjunanyi, ka Alitjinya ka:rkararingu kangkuru rawa wangkanyangka, munu kulingka kunyu pilupiluringangi.

''Awarinatju, wanyunatju puta tjintjulu mantjila,'' munu kunyu uranu mununku mangkangka tjintjulu wakaningi, ka wati wirtjapakanu malu, watjara, ''Awari, awarinatju, malaringuna.'' Ka wanyu kulila, malu paluru piranpa—piranpa alatjitu. Munu kunyu iluru-ilururira yakutja wana kulu witira ma-tarararira pitingka tjarpangu. Ka tjitji panya kungkangku nyakula urulyarara pakara wananu, munu ma-wanara pitingka tjarpangutu, piruku pakantjikitjangku kulilwiya alatjitu. Munu kunyu tjarpara piti unngu ankula ankula punkanu, munu kunyu rawa punkaningi kulira, ''Ngati pulka manti nyangatja, munta, ngati wiya, purkarana punkani.'' Munu paluru tjaruringkula para-nyangangi, munu walu-nyangangitu, palu putu kunyu nyangangi marungka, piti panya unngu.

Down the Hole

Alitji was getting very tired of sitting in the creek-bed. She and her sister had been playing milpatjunanyi, a story-telling game. They each had a stick and a pile of leaves, and took it in turn to tell a story about their family. The sandy ground was their stage; the leaves were the people. As they told the stories, each softly tapped her stick in time to the rhythm of her rising and falling voice, and every now and then they would sweep the sand smooth with the backs of their hands.

Alitji had become very bored as her sister's voice went on and on, and her eyelids began to droop. ''Well,'' she said to herself, ''perhaps I'll collect some tjintjulu berries to decorate my hair.'' This she did, and then began to pierce the berries with small sticks, and poke them through the strands of her hair.

Suddenly a kangaroo hopped past her, saying, ''Oh dear, oh deary me, I'm late.'' And the extraordinary thing was that he was white. A white kangaroo! He hurried on anxiously, clutching a dilly-bag and a digging-stick, and disappeared from view down a hole in the ground. In great surprise, Alitji jumped up and followed him, the tjintjulu berries bouncing about her head; down she went into that hole in the ground, never stopping to think how she would get out again.

Alitji and her sister were playing in a creek-bed when a white kangaroo hopped past and disappeared into a hole in the ground.

Alitjinya pula kangkurura karungka inkangi ka malu piranpa wirkara pitingka tjarpara wiyaringu.

Ka ngarangilta lau tjukutjuku tjutangka mai kutjupa kutjupa, ka Alitjilu punkara marangku lau kutjunguru mantjinu piti tjanmatatjara, palu mai muntu mulyararira ngalkuwiyangku wantingu, munu marangku kanyiningi punkatjingaliangku anangu kutjupa tjaru nyinantja winyulpungkuntjaku-tawara. Munu kunyu rawa ukalingkula piti malakungku tjunu, lau kutjupangka.

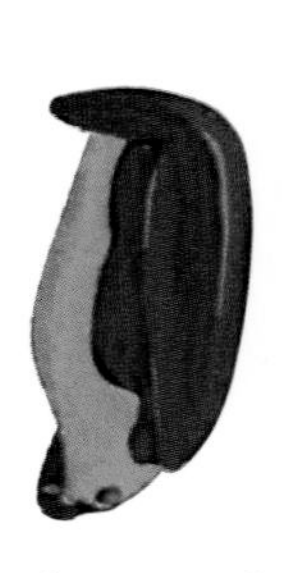
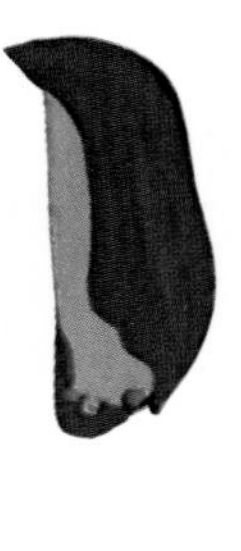

"Kakari punkaninatju alatjitu. Ngati nyangatja putu kulintja. Panya itara katunguruna punkara tjukutjukunmankuku palu nyangatja ngati ngurpatja." Munu wangkara tjaruringkula wirkankuwiyatu palurunku wangkangi: "Kana ya:ltjingka wanyu ma-wirkankuku. Ngayulu tjinguru pana winkingka waintaringkula ilkari kutjupangka wirkankuku, mununtina tjintu kutjupalta nyakuku, pana nyangangka munkara. Kantiya anangu tjutalta kata kampa kutjuparira para-ngaraku ngura kampa kutjupampa. Kana ya:ltjingara tjanala wangkama? Ngayulu kulu manti kampa kutjupariku." Alatji tjitji paluru wirkankuwiyatu rawa alatjitu punkara punkara piruku wangkarinangi.

"Katju putjimpa? Watjilarinyi tjinguru, ngaltutjara. Ka palunya nganalu paltjalku? Awa putji putitja ṅya:kunanta

Inside the hole, she went on for some distance, then suddenly began to fall, and went on falling for a long time. She thought it must be a very, very deep hole, but then she decided: "No, not so deep, perhaps; it's only that I am falling very, very slowly."

And as she fell, Alitji looked about her. She couldn't see anything below her, for it was too dark. But in small depressions in the wall she could see different kinds of food. There was a dish of bulbs called tjanmata, which were very good to eat. She took a handful of these as she fell past them, but they weren't ripe; sulkily she decided she couldn't eat them, and for fear of hitting someone below, she held them in her hand until she was able to replace them in another depression as she fell past it.

"Goodness, I really am falling a long way," she thought. "This hole must be deep beyond imagination. In future, if I fall from the top of a gum tree, I'll think it's nothing compared with this." And so saying, she continued getting lower and lower without arriving anywhere, and began to talk to herself. "I wonder what I'll be coming to? I must fall right through the earth soon, and then I shall come to some other atmosphere. I suppose I'll see a different sun, out beyond this earth. And there might even be people—people who walk upside-down, perhaps, in that other-side place. How shall I speak to them? Perhaps I'll be upside-down, too!" Thus the child spoke to herself as she fell, still without arriving anywhere. She just kept on falling and talking.

"What about my cat? Pining for me, probably, the dear little thing. And who will feed her? Oh, pussy dear,

Alitji fell for a very long time until she landed suddenly in a heap of dry leaves.

Alitjinya rawa mulapa ukalingkula punkanu alatjitu untjuntjungka.

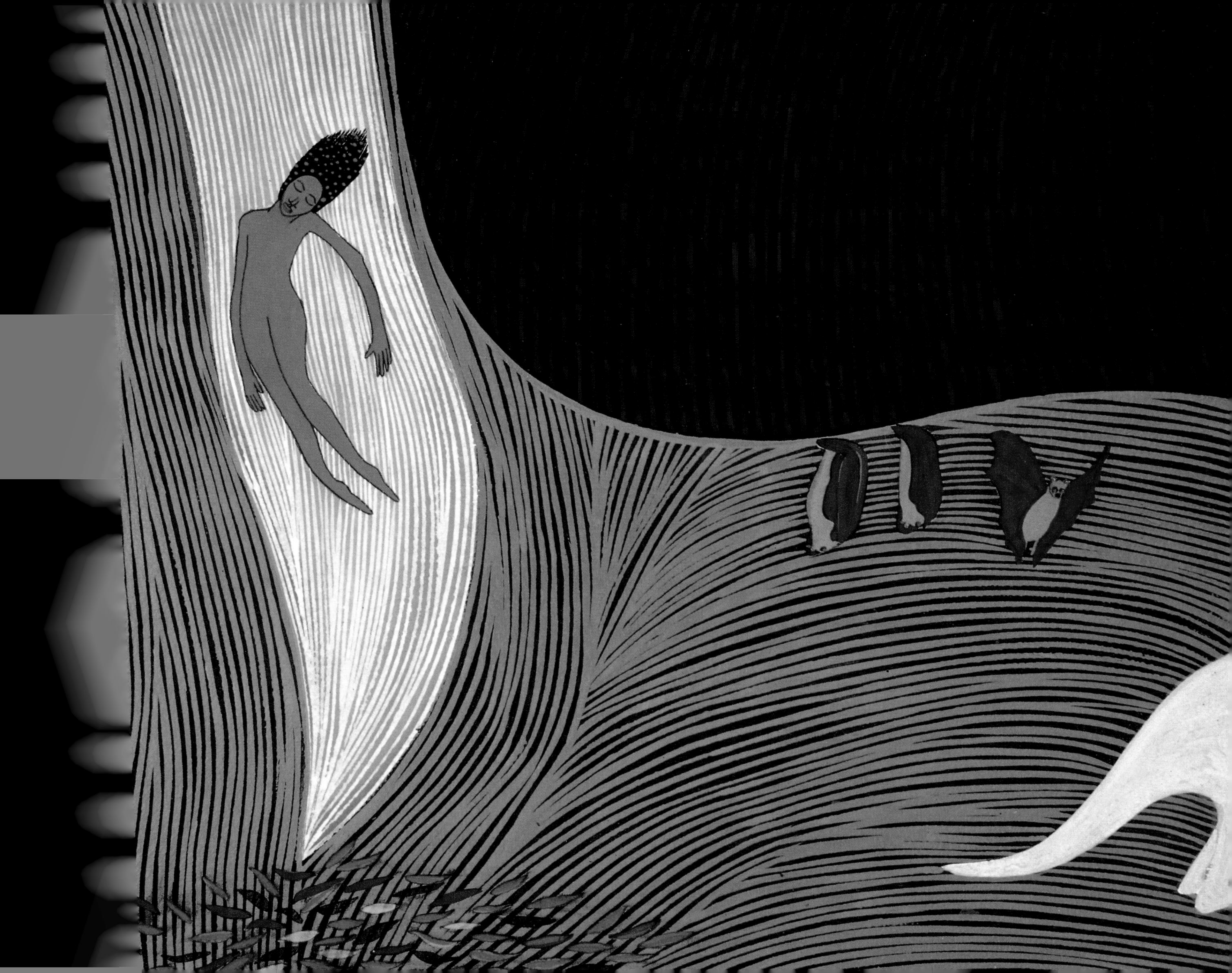

wantikatingu? Palu nyangangka wiya ngaranyi nyuntu ngalkuntjaku, tjulpu wiya, linga wiyatu, munta minga wiyatu. Nya:kuna linga wangkanyi, munta minga, linga, minga. Nya: putjingku ngalkupai? Minga? Wanyu, munta, mingangku putji ngalkupai. Wiya, awa putingku minga ngalkupai, minga wiya, linga ngalkupai.''

Munu alatji ngunti-ngunti wangkara wangkara kunkunarira tjukurmanu. Alatji kunyu ukalingkula tjukurmanu: mara witira pula anangi, Putji pula Alitjinya, ka watjanu Alitjilu, ''Putji putitja, mulamulangkuni wangka, nyuntu wanyu minga ngalkupai? Tjukarurungkuni wanyu wangka.'' Munu alatji wangkara punkanu alatjitu, untjuntjungka punkara ngaringi, ka ukalingkuntja wiya, tjitji paluru rawa punkantjatjanu mala mulapa wirkanu.

Alitjinya pika wiya wirkanu, munu mapalku pakanu munu ira-nyakula maru kutju nyangu, panya pana unngu nyaratja, ka kunyu kuranyu piti kutjupa wara mulapa ngarangi ka palula ma-tarararingi Malu Piranpa yakutjatjara, wanatjara. Ka kulinu Alitjilu, wangkanyangka, ''Awarinatju, malaringanyina, awari.'' Ka kunyu wangkara kampa kutjupa wanu para-pitjala wiyaringu, ka Alitjinya ma-wanara ala lipingka, kulpi purunytja wirkanu, palu wiya ngarangi Malu Piranpa, ka putu nyangu Alitjilu. Ka ala nyanga lipingka pintjantjara tjuta katu ngarangi. Ka tjitjingku para-nyakula ala utju tjuta katu ngaranyangka nyangu, munu paluru tji:lpa pulkangka tatira, ngura wiru mulapa kurungku nyangu ma-nyirkira, ala utju wanungku, ''Ngangari pika wiru alatjitu, palu ya:ltjingarana ma-pakalku? Ala nyangatja tjuku mulapa kana ngayulu tjitji pulka.'' Munu kunyu tjiturutjitururira para-ngarangi, munu kantunu kutjupa— ''Nya: wanyu palatja?'' Munu wana nyangu, ''Ngangari!''

why did I leave you behind? However, there's nothing here for you to eat, not a bird, not a lizard—no, I don't mean that, I should have said, not a gizzard. Why did I say lizard? I should have said gizzard for lizard . . . gizzard, lizard. What do cats eat? Gizzards? No, that's wrong—do gizzards eat cats? No, of course not. Cats eat gizzards—no, not gizzards, lizards . . .''

So Alitji went on dreamily talking nonsense to herself until she fell asleep. And then as she fell she dreamt. She dreamt that she and her cat were walking along hand-in-paw and that she was saying, ''No, seriously, pussy dear, do you eat gizzards? Tell me truly.'' And just as Alitji said this, she landed suddenly on a heap of dead leaves. After the long descent the fall was over.

Alitji was not a bit hurt; she jumped up in a moment. She looked up, but it was all dark overhead. In front of her lay another long passage. In it the White Kangaroo was still in sight, hurrying along with his dilly-bag and digging-stick, and Alitji could hear him saying, ''Oh dear, it's getting so late. Oh, deary me.'' She saw him disappear round a corner, and, following him, found herself in a large area like a cave. The White Kangaroo was nowhere to be seen, so Alitji began to look around her.

It was a large underground cave, with bats hanging from the roof and a number of small openings high on the walls, leading outwards. By climbing on to a large root, Alitji was able to peer through one of the openings into the beautiful world outside.

''Oh, what a lovely place,'' she said to herself. ''But how can I get out there? I'm such a big girl and these openings are so narrow.'' She climbed down and wandered sadly about. Suddenly she stumbled on

Munu mantjira, tji:lta tatira ala panyatja tjawara lipiningi.

Munu kunyu tjawara tjawara wana panyangka putu alatjitu lipinu, pana panya witu mulapa. Munu ukalingu munu piruku kunyu tjiturutjitururingu. ''Awarinatju ngura palatja ngangari itjanu alatjitu, inuntji yantji, ukiri lipi wanu, uru kulukulu ngaranyi kana unngu nyanga marungka nyinanyi alatjitu.''

Munu kunyu nyangu kampurarpa munu mantjinu kulira, ''Nyangatja nganmanpa wiya ngarangi.'' Munu kunyu nyangangi, ''Mai wanyu nyangatja? Kampurarpa palya wanyu? Panya tjitji kutjupa tjutaya tjuni pikaringkupai muntu ngalkula.''

Palu nyakula arkara palyanmara ngalkunu, kampurarpa kuru wiru. Palu ngalkula kunyu tjitji paluru mutumuturingu munu palya ngarangi ala panyangka tjarpantjikitja, palu ngarala pataningi, piruku tjukutjukuringkuntjaku-tawara, ''Tjinguruna kuwari tjukutjukuringkula wiyaringanyi tili purunypa. Palu tili wiyaringkuntja nya: purunypa? Wampanti, ngayulu nyakuwiya tili wiyaringkuntja. Nya: purunyarikuna

something. ''A digging-stick! Just what I need.'' And she climbed again on to the root and began to dig at the opening to enlarge it. But the ground was so hard that after a great deal of digging she had made little headway. Greatly discouraged, she climbed down again. ''What a shame, it looks so beautiful out there. The grass is full of wild flowers, and I'm sure there would be witchety grubs in those cassias. And here am I, shut up in this miserable dark place.''

Walking back, Alitji noticed, this time, some wild tomatoes. ''They weren't here before,'' she said, looking at them closely. ''Are they really good to eat? I've known several children who got bad pains from eating wild tomatoes that weren't properly ripe.''

She tasted one carefully before finishing them all. No sooner had she eaten the last one than she found herself getting shorter and shorter. In no time she was small enough to be able to crawl through one of the openings, but she stood quite still just where she was, wondering if she would disappear altogether, like a flame. ''But what does a flame look like when it has gone wanyu?'' Palu wiya, Alitjinya piruku tjukutjukuringkuwiya nyinangi munu wiyaringkuwiyatu wirtjapakanu pukularira, ala panya wanu ma-pakantjikitja. Palu awari, panya anga ngarangi tji:lpa pulka, ka putulta tatinu, tjitji panya tjuku mulapa. Palu arkara arkara putu alatjitu tatinu, punu palatja wirulywirulypa alatjitu, ka pakuringkula nyinakatira ulangu. Ngaltutjara.

''Wanti, ula wiyangku, tjitji ulanti nyuntu. Wiyariwa awa!'' Alatji tjitji Alitjilunku painu. Tjakangku kunyu tjitji palurunku payiningi mununku kutjupa arangku pungu nguntjungka tungunpungkula, anangu, kutjara palku nyinara.

Munu tjiturutjituru nyinara nyangu yakutja ngarinyangka, munu watjanu, ''Muntauwa! Malu Pirantu nyangatja wala pulka ankula punkatjinganu.'' Munu alara nyangu unngu ngarinyangka mai panya witita. Munu paluru, tjuku mulatu yakutjangka tjarpara witita mantjinu munu ngalkunu tjukutjuku, munu mara katangka arkara tjunu wararingkunyangka pampuntjikitjangku. Palu wiya—kutjupariwiya—Alitjinya palurutu nyinangi ngalkulatu. ''Muntauwa, nya:kuna kutjuparintjikitjangku kulinu? Palu awa, ngura nyangangka tjuta mantu kutjuparinyi, kana piruku kutjuparintjikitjangku kulinu. Tjaka mantu, ngura nyangangka.'' Munu alatji kulira witita ngalkula wiyanu, mai wiru.

out?'' she thought. ''I have never seen such a thing. I wonder what I shall look like?'' However, Alitji had by now stopped getting smaller, and she ran happily back towards the little opening she had peered through before.

Alas for poor Alitji! Blocking the opening was the enormous root, and now that she was so small she couldn't possibly climb it. She tried desperately, but its surface was too smooth, and presently, tired out, she sat down and began to cry. The poor little thing!

''Now stop that. You're just a cry-baby. Stop it at once,'' Alitji chided herself. She often gave herself a good talking-to, and had once even hit herself for disobeying her mother when they were out digging for honey-ants. She liked to pretend she was two people.

While Alitji was sitting there sadly, she noticed a dilly-bag lying on the ground. ''Goodness, the White Kangaroo must have dropped it as he hurried along,'' she said to herself. She opened it and saw yams inside. Alitji was so small that she had to crawl inside to reach them. She took a handful, crawled back out of the bag and nibbled a little, holding her hand on top of her head to feel which way it was growing. She was surprised to find that she stayed the same height. ''Well, why did I expect to change size?'' she thought. ''One doesn't usually after eating yams, but really, in this place so many strange things have happened that one expects them all the time.'' So she set to work and soon ate up the rest of the yams.

Alitji was so small, she had to crawl into the dilly bag to reach the yams.

Alitjinya tjuku mulapa yakutjangka tjarpangu wititaku.

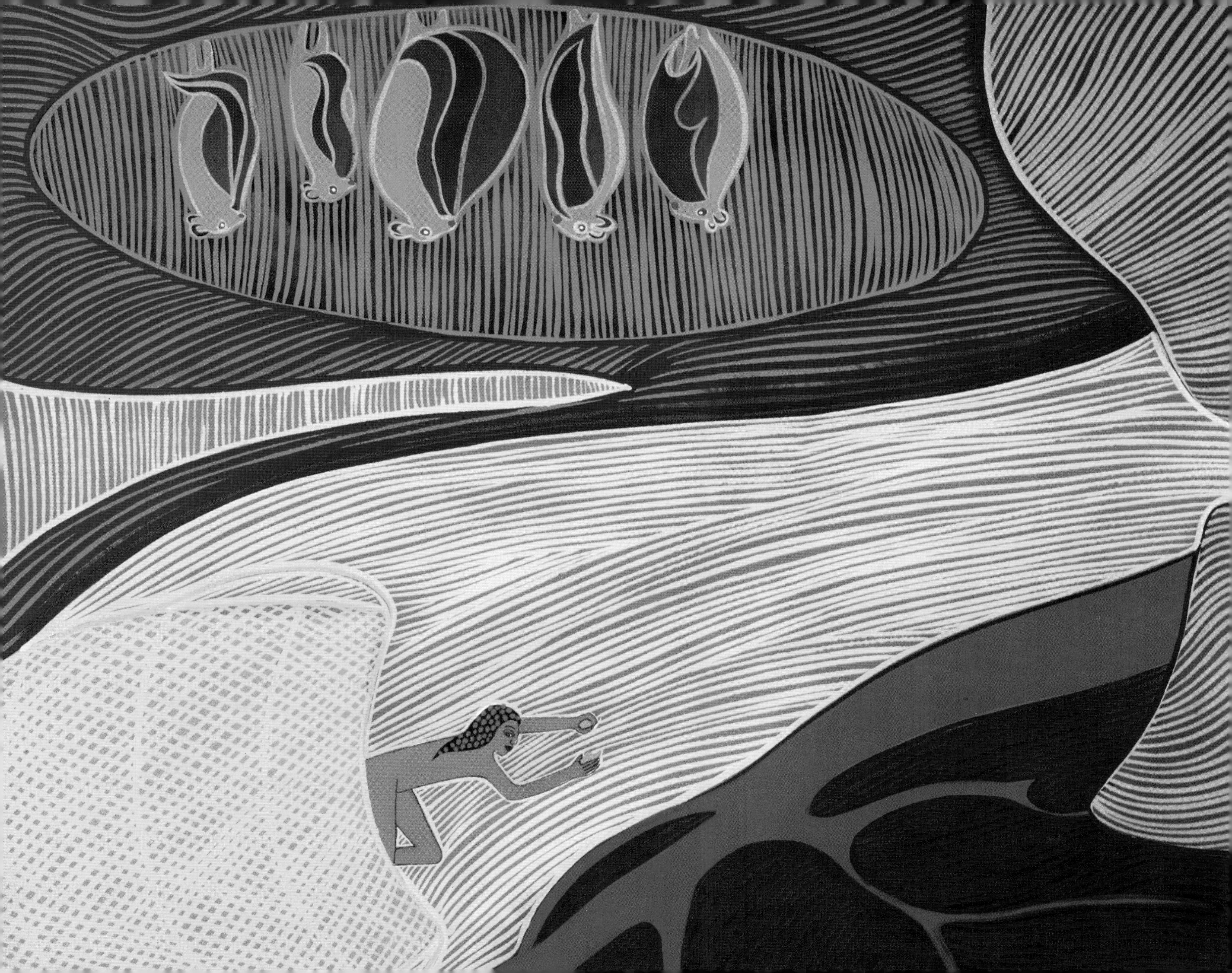

Ilantja Tjarpantja

"*Ala nyangatja*, pirukunatju wararinganyi. Tjina nyarana ma-wiyaringanyi kana kata nyanga katuringanyi alatjitu." Mununku tjina kunyu walu-nyakula putu nguwanpa nyangu, parari mulapa, munu kunyu watjilaringu. "Awa tjina putitja, nganalu nyupalinya kanyilku? Ngayulu mantu parariringu, mununa nyupalinya patungku putu atunymananyi. Wanyuna puta ngalturiwa, nyara pula parapitjaliangku wantintjaku-tawara, kana ya:ltjingara para-pitjama pula wantinyangkampa? Wanyu pula ngalya-kulila, mulapa ngayulu nyupalinya atunmara untjunmankuku warungka, mununa tjilka mantjilku wakanyangka. Mulamulangkuna wangkanyi, watarkuriwiyangku ngayulu nyupalinya kanyilku patungkutu." Munu kunyu alatji wangkantjatjanungku Alitjilunku kulinu, "Awari kata kawakawaringanyina, tjinangkanatju nya:ku wangkanyi" Munu katangku pungu katu, rawa panya wararingkula, munu pukularira tji:lpa panya pulkakutu wirtjapakara tatinu mapalku, palu awari pulkaringkula putu alatjitu ma-tjarpangu ala panya utjungka. Munu pupara ma-nyirkingi ngura panya ngarurpa, munu nyakula, mukuringkula nyinakatira piruku ulangi.

"Wanti, nya:kun ulanyi? Tjitji pulka mulapa nyuntu" (mulapa paluru pulka alatjitu) "munu nyuntu uti wantima ulawiyangku. Wanti! Mapalku wiyariwa!" Alatji tjitji palurunku painu. Palu wiyaringku-wiyatu rawa ulangi

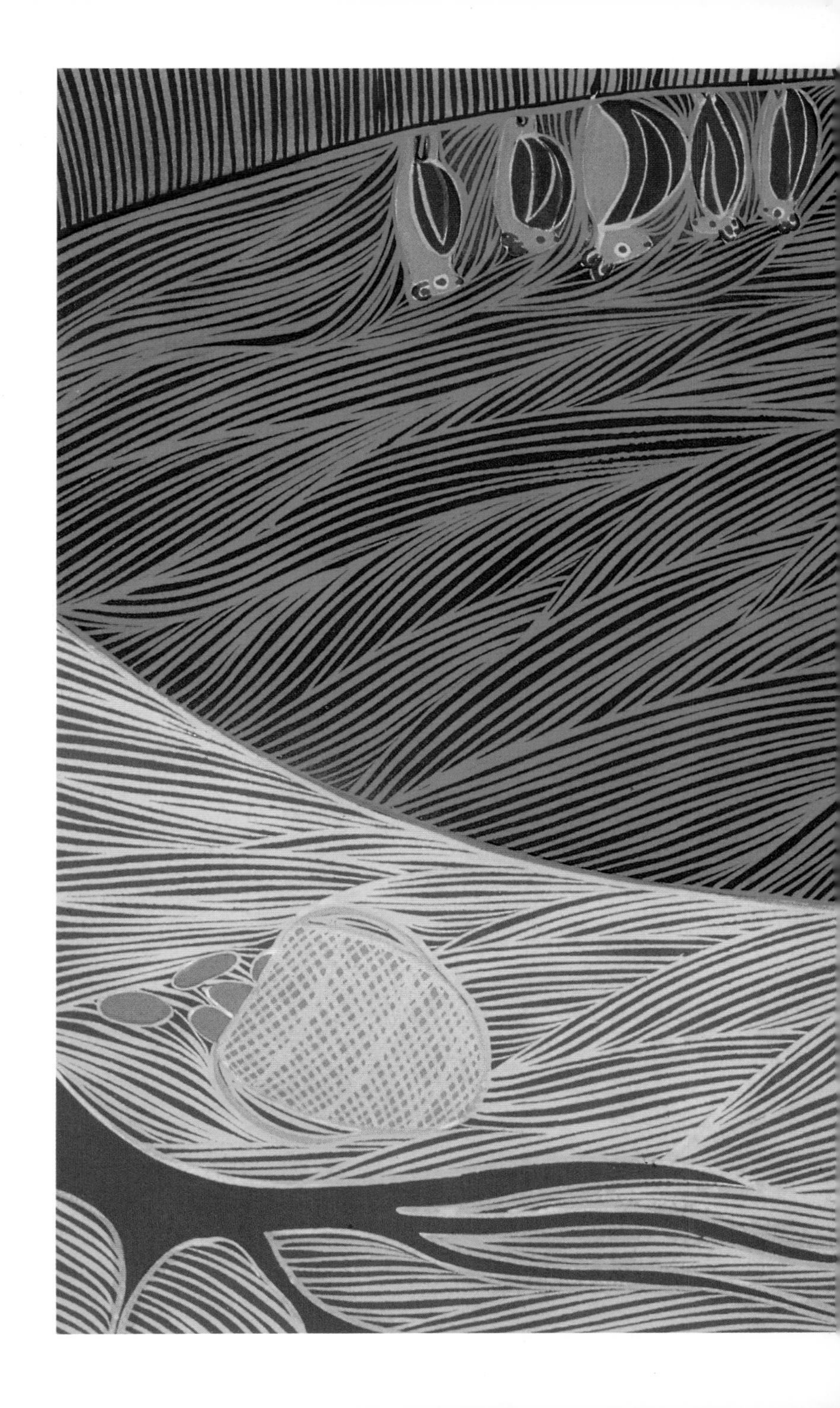

The Pool of Tears

"Well now, here I am growing tall again. My head is getting higher and higher and there go my feet, away in the distance. I can scarcely see them!" Alitji missed them sadly and called, "Dear feet, who will care for you? I am so far away and there you are, alone." Then she thought, "I'd better show them some sympathy, in case they refuse to carry me about, and then how should I manage?—Listen, my dears, somehow I will be able to look after you, to warm you by the fire and pull out prickles that get into your soles. Indeed I will not forget you, though I am so far away." And then she said, "Oh dear, what nonsense I'm talking. What is this I'm saying to my feet?"

At that moment her head struck the roof of the cave, and she hurried off to the big root and clambered on to it. But poor Alitji, she was now far too big to fit through the small opening; all she could do was to stoop down and peep through it into the beautiful bush beyond. She began to cry again.

"Now stop that! Why are you crying? A big girl like you"—she was indeed big—"you'd better stop at once, *at once*, do you hear!" Thus Alitji spoke severely to herself. But she really couldn't stop crying, and went on shedding enormous tears which dripped on to her legs and slipped down to the ground all around her, until there was a large pool almost covering the floor.

After eating the yams Alitji grew so big her head hit the roof of the cave and she started to cry.

Mai witita ngalkula Alitjinya wararingu mumunku kata katu pungkula piruku ulangi.

putu wantira, ka ilanypa tjutingi, ka pana ururingu, winki kunyu ururingu, tjitji panya pulka rawa ulanyangka.

Ka kulinu Alitjilu munmurpa ilaringkunyangka munu ilanypa wiyaringkula nyangu Malu Piranpa malaku pitjanyangka, miru kulunypa kanyira marangku. Munu walawala pitjala watjaningi tjuta arangku, "Awarinatju, payilkuni pulkara malaringkunyangka, pulkarani payilku patara patara, awarinatju."

Palu Alitjinya kunyu pakuringu unngu rawa nyinara, munu alpamilantjaku tjapintjikitjangku kuliningi. Ka Malu watarku ilaringu, tjitji kungka nyakuwiya, ka watjanu, Alitjilu, "Awa ngana . . ." purkarangku kunyu wangkangu palu Malu Piranpa pulkara urulyarara lanpurpungkula ma-wirtjapakanu wala pulka.

Ka Alitjilunku pakara miru mantjira watjanu, "Awari, uwankara kuwari kutjuparinyi. Panya mungartji uwankara palu purunypatu ngarangi, ka nya:ringu awa? Ngayunya tjinguru mungangka kutjupanu." Munu kunyu wangkara unytjungku miru kulunypa kanyiningi munu piruku tjitji palurunku milpatjura wangkangi: "Wanyu ngananya ngayulu pakanu mungawinki? Muntauwa, mulapa ngayulu tjitji kutjupa mungawinki wankaringu. Palu ngananyanatju puta wanyu? Putunatju papulananyi." Munu kunyu tjitji kutjupa tjuta, palumpa ngalungku kuliningi, palurunku ngurkananku ntjikitjangku.

"Wiya, ngayulu Ngintjanya wiya. Panya paluru mangka nyutirnyutirpa, ka ngayulu wiya, mununa Maringkanya wiyatu, tjitji paluru ngurpa alatjitu, kana ngayulu nintipuka. Awari, ngayulu kulu mantu ngurparingu, mununa tjuta putu kulini. Wanyunatju

After a time, Alitji heard footsteps approaching. She dried her tears and saw the Kangaroo returning, with a miniature woomera in his hand. He was hurrying towards her, muttering over and over again, "Oh, won't I be in trouble for being late again. Oh, she ***will*** be savage after waiting and waiting."

Alitji was so tired of being shut inside the cave that she decided to ask the Kangaroo for help. So when he came near, still without having noticed her, she said quietly, "I wonder, could . . ."

The Kangaroo started violently, threw down his woomera and with great leaps hopped away.

Alitji took up the woomera and said, "How queer everything is today. Yesterday things were just as usual. Perhaps I've been changed in the night."

As she spoke, she held the woomera and began to consider, in the usual way for little Aboriginal girls, what could have happened. Tapping the small woomera on the ground with one hand, she drew figures in the dust with her other hand, crooning softly to herself. "Let me think, was I the same when I got up this morning? Yes, I do remember feeling a bit different; who could I have become? I really don't recognize myself." And Alitji began to think over other girls she knew who were the same age as herself, to see if she could have been changed into any of them.

"I'm sure I'm not Ngintja, for her hair is curly and mine is not; and I'm certainly not Maringka, she's so ignorant, while I know such a lot; though I do seem to be getting very muddled today. I'd better test myself. I'll start with places I know. Let me see, Itjinpiri is to the

The White Kangaroo was startled when he saw Alitji in the cave.

Malu Piranpa urulyaranu Alitjinya kulpingka nyakula.

arkara ngura warara wangka. Itjinpirinya wilurara ngaranyi ka Wamikatanya ulparira, ka Wilunya punungka, palu Ulurunya karungka ngaranyi. Awari, putu nguwanpana kulini, ngunti-nguntina ngura wangkanyi, mulapa ngayulu pina patiringu. Wanyuna puta inma inka.'' Munu alatji inma inkangu:

Ngintaka kanpi panyatja
Wipu wiruringu
Munu kuka nganmanitja
Pulkara wantingu

Pukultju ikaringkula
Tjinangku witira
. Antipina ku:ltjunkula
Tjuni tja:lyngarangu.

west and Wamikata to the south, while Wilu is among the trees and Uluru is on the creek. Oh, dear, I can't really remember, I'm sure I'm mixing everything up, I'm getting quite lost. I'll try a song.'' And she began to sing about the perenti, a kind of large goanna. The title of the song was *Ilili nyampulnyampul:*

How doth the little perenti
Improve his shining tail,
And sup a little differently
By never eating quail!

How cheerfully he seems to grin,
How neatly spreads his claws,
And welcomes little fishes in
With gently smiling jaws!

Alatji ngunti inkangi tjitji panya paluru inma nyangatja. Ka tjukurpa kutjuparingu, ka putu playanu Alitjilu, munu ilanypa piruku pakanu. Munu watjanu, "Muntauwa, mulapa ngayulu Maringkanya nyinanyi mununa palumpa nguntjungka puta nyinama. Awari kura alatjitu, ngayulu wantinyi, minyma una mantu paluru, mununa ngura nyangangka unngu palya titutjara nyinaku. Altikuniya malaku ankuntjaku, palu wiya, tjungunpungkulana rawa nyangangka nyinaku. Mulapa ngayulu Maringkaku nguntjuku kuraringanyi. Minyma kata ultu palurunku. Palu awari—utiya pitjala ngayunya altima; mulapa ngayulu ngura nyanga unngutja wantinyi; lutju nyinarana pakuringu alatjitu mununa watjilarinyi." Munu tjitji paluru pupakatira ulangu piruku.

Palu pupakatira Alitjilunku tjina nyangu, ila mulapa. "Munta, pirukuna tjukutjukuringu." Munu kunyu pakara wirtjapakanu tji:lpakutu, palu rawatu tjitji paluru tjukutjukuringangi munu kulinu, "Awa mirungkuni wiyani," munu palunya punkatjinganu watalpi wiyaringkula. "Awarinatju tjuku mulararinguna. Palya, kuwarina ala utjungka mapalku tjarpaku." Palu wiya, tji:lpa panya pulka anga ngarangi ka tjukutjukuringkula

Alitji sang all the wrong words; she couldn't get it right, and the tears again welled up in her eyes. "It's true, I know nothing. I really must be Maringka after all, and that means I'll have to live with her mother. I don't like her mother at all—she never brings home enough wood to keep the family warm. If I'm Maringka, then I'll stay down here and never go home at all. They can call me for as long as they like, I shall just disobey. I don't like Maringka's mother one bit, she's so empty-headed." Then—"Oh, dear," cried Alitji with a sudden burst of tears, "I wish they would come and call me home. I'm so very tired of being inside this stuffy place all alone."

Alitji, as she said this, noticed that her feet were again much closer. "I'm small again!" she declared. Jumping up, she ran back towards the opening, but suddenly realized that she was still shrinking rapidly.

"Goodness," she said, "it's the woomera that's causing this." She dropped it hastily, just in time to prevent herself from shrinking away altogether. "That was a narrow escape," she thought. "And now for that beautiful place."

putulta tatinu. Ngaltutjara, tjinguru paluru titutjara nyinaku piti nyara palula, pana unngu.

Palu ma-pitjala kunyu wirulyarara punkanu urungka, munu kulinu, "Ngangari, tjintjirangkana tjarpangu." Palu wiya, tjitji palurunku ilanytja punkanu, panya nganmanpa paluru tjitji wara witjinti purunypa ulangi, ka ilanypa pulka tjutingu ka ururingu. Pala palula Alitjinya punkanu, munu urungka para-pitjala piwiyaringkula watjanu, "Utina ulawiyangku wantima, kuwarinatju tjitji tjukutjuku ilanytja karalukatinyi rawa ulantjatjanu."

Munu kunyu urungka para-pitjala tjalapungkunyangka kulinu, munu ilaringu nyakuntjikitja, kalaya palku kulira, munta, kanyala-tjinguru, palu wiya. Panya Alitjinya tjukutjukuringu, ka palatja mingkiringku tjalapungangi. Paluru kulukulu wirulyarara tjarpangu.

Ka Alitjinya mukuringu palula wangkantjikitja, alatji kulira, "Mingkiri manti wangkapai, ngura nyangangka panya uwankara kampa kutjuparingu." Munu watjanu alatji: "Mingkiri, nyuntu wanyu ninti? Ya:ltjingkali uru nyanganguru pakalku? Rawana para-pitjala para-pitjala pakuringu, awa Mingkiri?"

Alitjilu alatji Mingkiringka wangkantjikitjangku kulinu palu Mingkiringku ngapartji wangkawiyangku nyangangi kutju.

"Muntauwa, Pitjantjatjaraku ngurpa manti. Wati piranpa tjinguru pitjangu, ngura nyanga kutu, wanyuna puta Ingkilitja wangka." Munu watjanu Mingkiringka, *"Where is the dog?"* (Alitjilu tjukurpa nyangaku kulangka nintiringu.)

Ka Mingkiri tjirkara ma-wararakatingu munu panangka nyinara tjititingangi.

She ran towards the opening, but of course she found that once again she was too small to climb on to the root to reach it. The poor child; it looked as though she would be in this dismal hole for ever.

In trying to climb on to the root, Alitji's foot slipped. *Splash!* she was up to her neck in salt water. At first she thought she was in a deep claypan, but soon realized she was in the pool of tears she had cried when she was as big as a corkwood tree. How she regretted all that crying now, as she swam and swam trying to get out! "I wish I hadn't cried so much. It looks as though I shall drown in my own tears."

Just then she heard a splashing and swam towards a large creature in the water, thinking that it must be an emu, or perhaps a hill kangaroo, but then she remembered how small she had become, and soon made out that it was only a Hopping Mouse that, like herself, had slipped into the pool.

Alitji decided to speak to the Hopping Mouse, thinking, "No doubt it can talk—in this place everything is topsy-turvey." So she said, "Hopping Mouse, do you know how we can get out of this pool? I am very tired of swimming about here, please, Hopping Mouse."

But the Hopping Mouse answered nothing.

"I see," she thought. "It doesn't speak English, so I'd better try Pitjantjatjara." And she tried again: *"Papa ya:ltji?"* (This was the first sentence in her Pitjantjatjara lesson book. It meant: "Where is the dog?")

No sooner had Alitji spoken these words than the Hopping Mouse made a sudden leap out of the water and quivered all over with fright.

Alitji, now small again, found herself swimming in a pool of her own tears — and so was a Hopping Mouse.

Alitjinya tjukutjukuringkula uru ilanytjanku tjarpangu — ka Mingkiri kulu ilanytja.

Ka kuntaringkula watjanu Alitjilu, ''Munta, nyuntu papa wantipai, utina papa wankawiyangku wantima.''

''Papa wantipai mantu ngayulu! Nyuntu wanyu mingkiririra papaku mukuringkuku?'' Alatji Mingkiringku mirpanarira watjanu.

Ka watjanu Alitjilu, ''Wiya mantu, palu mirpanpa wiyariwa. Palu awari, utinanta nganampa papa nyuntula nintila. Patjalpai wiya paluru, pilunpa wiru, ngayuku malpa mulapa. Mulapa nyuntu nyakula palumpa mukuringkuku, ngaltuntju wiru paluru, munu warungka ngarira kunkunaripai, munu liru ngululpai, mingkiri kulu munta!'' Palu Mingkiri ngaltutjara, nyangatja kulira pakara tiwilaringu, ka Alitjilu piruku kuntaringkula watjanu, ''Munta, tjitji kurana, wanyulinku papa wangkawiyangku wantima.''

''Ngayulu mantu kuwaripatjara wantingu, ka nyuntu kutjungku wangkangi. Nganana uwankarangku waltja winkingku tjananya wantipai, kura tjuta.'' Alatji watjantjatjanu wipu winki tjititingkula Mingkiri urungka ma-pitjangu pulkara tjalapungkula.

''Oh,'' said Alitji, ''I'm so sorry, I forgot that I shouldn't talk about dogs to a Hopping Mouse. Of course you don't like them.''

''Certainly I don't like them. Would you, if you were a Hopping Mouse?'' he asked angrily.

''Perhaps not,'' Alitji answered. ''Don't be angry about it. Yet I wish you could see our dog. He's very quiet and never bites, and he's a wonderful kangaroo catcher. Once you saw him you couldn't help liking him, he's so quiet. He sleeps at our fire, and frightens off snakes and Hopping mi—oh, I'm sorry!''

The Hopping Mouse, poor thing, was bristling all over, and Alitji, much ashamed, said, ''I'm sorry—I'm so silly, let's not talk of dogs any more.''

''*I* never have,'' said the Hopping Mouse, ''you've been doing so all by yourself. My whole family has always hated them—nasty things.'' And having said this, trembling to the tip of his tail, the Hopping Mouse swam away from Alitji, making a great splashing.

Ka ma-altingu, purkarangku, "Mingkiri putitja, awa, ngalya-pitja. Mulapa ngayulu papa wangkawiyangku wantiku."

Ka kunyu kulira Mingkiri malaku pitjangu, munu Alitjila tjalymara watjanu, "Pana piltikutuli ma-pitja, kananta uwankara tjakultjunkuku."

Palya mantu pula urunguru pakanu. Uru paluru anganu alatjitu, tjulpu tjuta, kuka kulukulu palula punkanyangka—Urutja, Tutu, Luri, Lu:npa, Liru kulu urungka para-ngarangi, kutjupa tjutaya kulukulu.

Ka Alitjinya kuranyuringu kaya kutjupa uwankarangku wananu munuya pana piltingka ma-wirkanu.

Alitji called softly: "Hopping Mouse dear, do come back again, and we won't talk of dogs or cats."

When the Hopping Mouse heard this it came back and said in a low voice, "Let us get to the shore, and I'll explain to you why I hate cats and dogs."

It was a good thing they decided to go, because the pool had become quite crowded with birds and animals that had fallen into it: there was a duck, a dodo, a lory, a kingfisher, a python, and others besides, all swimming about.

Alitji led the way and they all went to the shore.

Piltiringkuntja Munu Tjukurpa Pulka

Ngaltutjara tjutaya pakanu urunguru, wintju alatjitu. Tjulpu tjutaya tjiturutjituru mulapa nyalpi kurakuratjara panangka nyinangi, kaya kuka tjuta inyu uru winki mirpanpa para-ngarala tjititingangi.

"Palu ya:ltjingarala piltiringkuku?" Nyangatjaya mapalku kulinu, ka Alitjinya tjana mapalku ngalutjuringu munuyanku rapangku wangkangi, "Ya:ltjingarala piltiringkuku? Palu ngananya wanyu ninti puka?"

Palu Langkangku watjanu, "Ngayuluna kuwaripatjara miri pilkiringu." Ka watjanu Lirungku, "Ngayuluna kulukulu. Pilki alatjitu ngayulu."

Kaya tjapinu kutjupa tjutangku, "Nya: nyupali wangkanyi? Pilki mantu nyupali. Palu ngananа inyu uru winkingku piltiringkuntjikitjangku kulini."

Ka watjanu Langkangku, "Muntauwa nyura kulukulu mukuringanyi pilkiringkuntjikitja."

Ka Mingkiringku, mayatjangku pakara mirara watjanu, "Nyinakatiya uwankara munu ngalya-kulila. Nyayuluna nyuranya pilkilku." Kaya mapalku nyinakatingu

Getting Dry and the Long Tale

They were indeed a miserable party that climbed out of the water, wet and bedraggled. The birds stood on the bank with drooping feathers and the animals shivered with their fur clinging close to them, cross and uncomfortable.

The first thing they all thought of was how to get dry. They began to discuss this among themselves and were soon talking confidently to each other, as though they were all old friends.

"Who is the wisest of us all?" someone asked.

"Well," said the Blue-tongued Lizard, "I have the most wrinkled skin. It has been wrinkled since the beginning of time."

"What do you mean?" the others asked. "What has that to do with it?"

"Wrinkles and wisdom go together, do they not?" said the Blue-tongued Lizard. "But still," he added sadly, "I'm not wise enough to be able to tell you how to get dry."

At last the Hopping Mouse, who seemed to be a person of authority among them, stood up and called out, "Sit down, all of you and listen to me. I'll soon make you dry enough."

They were indeed a miserable party that climbed out of the water, wet and bedraggled.

Ngaltutjara tjutaya wintju alatjitu urunguru pakanu.

mangurimanguri pulka, ka Mingkiri ngururpa ngarangu. Ka Alitjilu palunya iluruilururira nyangangi kulira "Mulapa ngayulu kuwari urkaltjararinganyi. Nyanga wari pulkana nyinanyi. Utina mapalku untjunarima."

Ka Mingkiringku kanankanantu alatji tjanala watjanu, "Kulilaya, wangkanyina ḳuwari nyura uwankara pilkiringkuntjaku. Pilunariya! Wanyuya uwankara pilunari! Kuwaripatjara mulapa nganana kuka uwankara miri pilki ngarangi, langka purunypa."

Ka watjanu Patiltu tjititingkula, "Kakari!"

Ka watjanu Mingkiringku kuraringkula palumpa, "Munta, wangkangu nyuntu?"

Ka watjanu Patiltu, "Wiyana."

Ka watjanu Mingkiringku, "Munta, ngunti mantina kulinu. Pilunariya! Munula uwankara nyalpi wiya, inyu wiyatu miri pilki alatjitu nyinangi. Munulanku miri pilkingku piriningi rawangku, munula purtjutja alatjitu nyinangi."

Ka watjanu Urutjangku, "Ngananya wanyu purtjutjara? Nganana wanyu, urutja tjutala?"

"Uwa mantu, uwankarala kuwaripatjara purtju winki nyinangi—Patilpa, Tutu, Urutja, Langka, Mingkiri uwankara alatjitu purtjutjara nyinangi."

Ka watjanu Urutjangku, "Palu nganngimpa? Ka kuyimpa? Ngayuluna panya nganngi ngalkupai. Purtjutjana wanyu ngalkuningi?"

Palu Mingkiringku kulilwiyangku palku rawangku wangkangi, "Munula wayawayaningi, ka pakanu tjintjira nguru liru kutjupa, liru inyutjara." Ka Mingkiringku malakukutura nyakula watjanu Alitjila, "Alitji, palyaringanyin? Pilkiringu nyuntu?"

They all sat down at once, in a large ring with the Hopping Mouse in the middle. Alitji watched him anxiously; she was sure she would catch a bad cold if she did not soon get warm.

"Listen," said the Hopping Mouse, with an important air, "I have something to say that will make us all dry. Everyone be quiet, all of you now, be quiet. In the very beginning we all had dry scaly skin, like the Lizard."

"Ugh," said the Port Lincoln Parrot with a shiver.

"I beg your pardon," said the Hopping Mouse, annoyed. "Did you speak?"

"Not I," said the Port Lincoln Parrot.

"I beg your pardon," said the Hopping Mouse again, "perhaps I was mistaken. Quiet, all. We were all without fur and feathers, our skin was scaly all over, and these scales began to itch, so we scratched ourselves until our skin became dry and peeled."

The Duck asked, "We all had this dry, peeling skin? Even the water birds such as myself?"

"Yes, certainly. All of us, at the beginning of time, were covered with it—Parrot, Dodo, Duck, Hopping Mouse, Lizard, everyone had dry, peeling skin."

The Duck interrupted again. "But what about frogs? And worms? I eat them, you know. Do you mean I ate them when they had this diseased skin?"

The Hopping Mouse pretended not to notice this question, and went on hurriedly, "And as we were all itching and tickling, a snake arose from a claypan, a fur-covered snake." And at this point the Hopping Mouse turned to Alitji and said, "How are you getting on now, my dear, is your skin drying?"

Alitji and the animals sat in a circle around the Hopping Mouse.

Kaya uwankara nyinakatingu manguri manguri pulka, ka Mingkiri ngururpa ngarangu.

"Ngayulu wintju alatjitu nyinanyi. Nyuntunin wangkara wangkara putu piltini."

Ka watjanu Tutungku, "Ala palatja, tjukurpa wantirala piltiringkuntjikitja para-wirtjapakanma."

"Ya:ltjingkala? Ngura nyangatja anganu kala nyanga tjuta nyinanyi." Alatji Lunpangku watjanu.

Ka piruku watjanu Tutungku, "Mangurimanguringkala uru kantiltja para-wirtjapakanma winaringkuntjikitja."

Kaya uwankara, kutjukutju urukutu ma-pitjala para-wirtjapakaningi, tjungu wiya. Kaya kutjupa tjarangku pakuringkula wantingi, kaya kutjupa tjara rawa para-wirtjapakaningi, uru pantangka. Ka uru panya ilanypa ngururpa kaya kuka tjuta, tjitji kungka Alitjinya, kulukulu para-wirtjapakaningi. Munuya wirtjapakantjatjanu piltiringu munuya akuruakururingu munuya ngalymanangi, ka mirara watjanu Tutungku, "Ala wiyaringu!" Kaya uwankarangku palulakutu tjungu ankula ngalyngalymara watjaningi, "Ngananya nganmanpa wirkanu? Ngananya winaringu?"

Palu Tutungku rawangku kulira kulira kutju ngula mulatu watjanu, tjana pilunpa patanyangka, "Uwankarala, kalanya uwankara puta uwa."

"Nganalulanya?" Tjutangkuya tjapinu, tjungungku.

"Paluru, mantu!" Alitjinya wilitjunkula watjanu Tutungku, kaya uwankarangku mapalku Alitjinya utjunu mirara, "Uwalanya! Uwalanya!"

Alitjinya kuntaringu, maralpa mirangka ngarala, mununku kulinu, "Awari nya:na tjananya ungkuku? Awari . . . muntauwa," munu tjintjulu panyanpa mangkanguru mantjira para-ungu.

Ka watjanu Mingkiringku, "Palu palumampa? Nya: ngaranyi palumpa?"

"I am as wet as ever," she replied. "All this talking doesn't dry me."

"That's right! Let's leave this story and run around—that's the way to get dry!" said the Dodo.

"Where? This place is very crowded, with the claypan over there and so many animals here." Thus spoke the Kingfisher.

The Dodo spoke again. "Let's have a race in a circle around the claypan."

So they all, one by one, went over to the edge of the claypan and began to run. They joined the race just when they liked and left off running whenever they chose, and after some time they were all dry. After some time longer they began to get hot, and to pant and puff. Suddenly the Dodo shouted, "It's over!" And they all crowded round him, saying, "Who won? Who won?"

This question the Dodo could not answer without a great deal of thought, and he considered carefully while the others waited. At last the Dodo said, "Everybody has won and all must have prizes."

"But who is to give the prizes?" they all asked together.

"Why, she is, of course," said the Dodo, pointing to Alitji; and the whole party at once crowded around Alitji, calling out, "Give us prizes, give us prizes!"

Alitji was very embarrassed to be standing before them empty-handed. "Oh dear, what can I give them?" she thought. "Why, of course!" And she began to pull the tjintjulu berries from her hair, and pass them round.

But the Hopping Mouse said, "And what about herself? What is there for her?"

It was the Dodo who suggested they all race around the claypan to get dry.

Tutungku watjanu mangurimanguringka para-wirtjapakantjaku piltiringkunt-jikitjangku.

Ka watjanu Tutungku ikaringkuwiyangku, "Nya: kutjupa nyuntu kanyini?" Ka Alitjilu tjiturutjiturungku ngapartji watjanu, "Nyangatja kutju, mingkulpa," munu pinanguru mantjinu.

Ka watjanu, "Uwani." Ka ungu Alitjilu, kaya tjulpu uwankara, kuka tjuta kulukulu piruku tjunguringkula ilaringu palula, ka Tutungku katu wangkangu tjutangka mirangka, "Mingkulpa nyangatja nganana nyuntunya unganyi, ka nyuntu pulitji wirungku mantjira kanyinma." Munu watjara ungu Alitjinya, mingkulpa palumpa alatjitu.

Ka ikaringkuwiyangku pupakatira mantjinu, alatji kulira, "Nyangatja uwankara kawakawa alatjitu."

Kaya kuwaritu uwankara nyinakatingu, munuyanku tjintjulu nyalpingka, inyungka kanankananarira wakaningi, palu Lirungku, Ngintakangku miri pilki tjutangku putu wakara ngalkunu—tjintjulu ngalkunu. Kaya kutjupa tjuta pukulpa nyinangi tjintjulutjara, munuyanku wirunmanangi.

Munuya wiyaringkula kuwaritu mangurimanguri piruku nyinakatingu, munuya Mingkiringka ngatjiningi tjukurpa kutjupa tjanala wangkantjaku.

Ka tjukurpa wara alatji watjanu.

The Dodo said gravely, "What else have you?"

"Only this," Alitji said, taking some tobacco, called mingkulpa, from behind her ear.

"Hand it over," said the Dodo.

Then all the birds and animals once again crowded around Alitji while the Dodo solemnly presented the mingkulpa to her, saying loudly, in front of them all, "We beg your acceptance of this very special mingkulpa."

Alitji did not dare to laugh; she bowed and received her own mingkulpa back again, thinking to herself, "This whole thing is quite absurd."

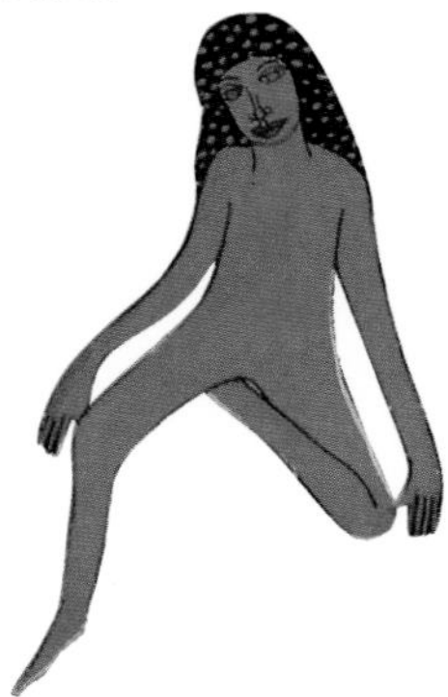

Immediately they all sat down, and the animals and birds began to decorate their fur and feathers with the tjintjulu berries, but the snakes and lizards complained that they could not use theirs in this way, so they ate them—yes, they actually ate the tjintjulu berries. The others were very happy and pleased with themselves and congratulated one another on their improved appearance.

When it was all finished they sat in a circle again and begged the Hopping Mouse to tell them something more. So the Mouse told them this long tale:*

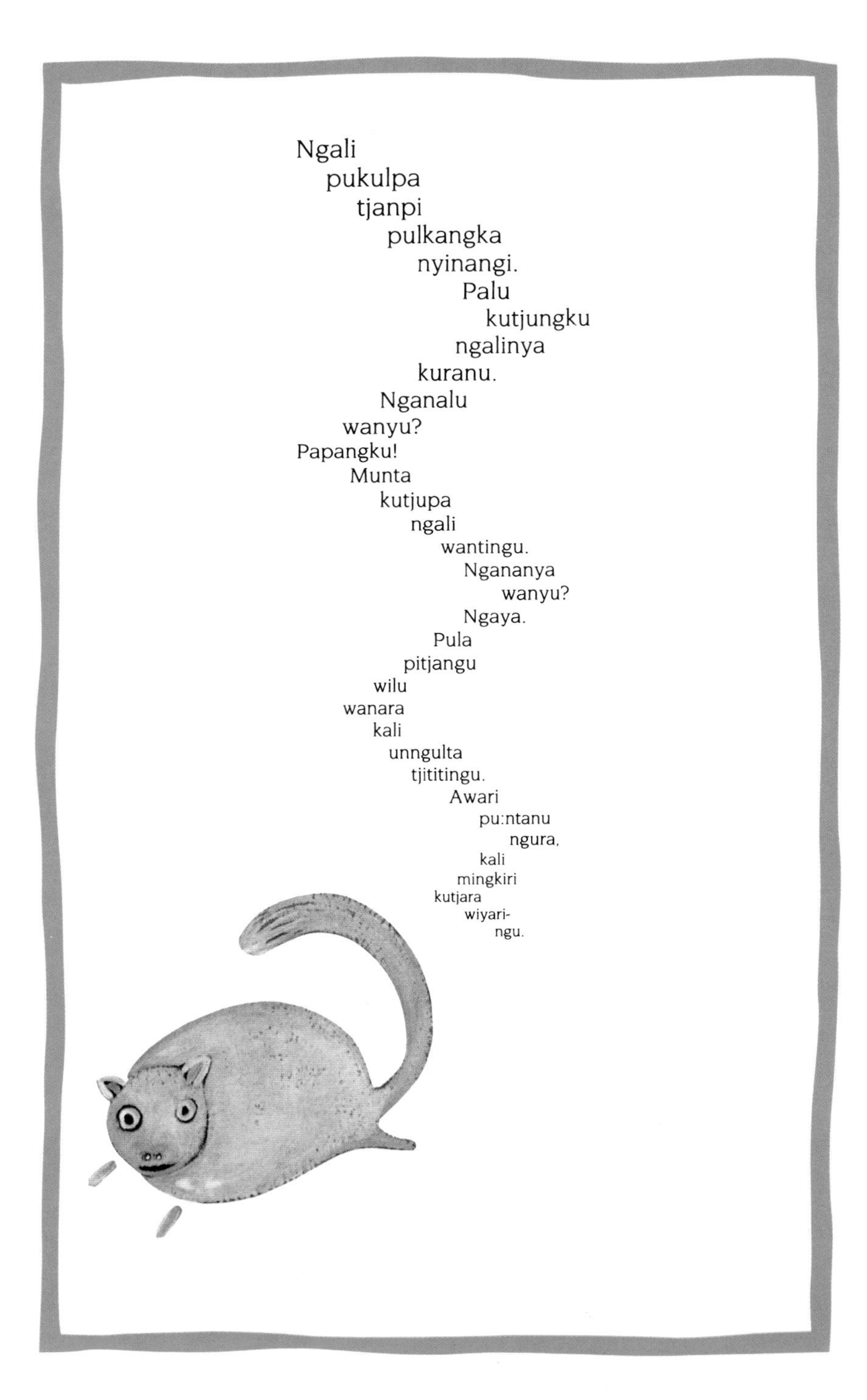

Ngali
pukulpa
tjanpi
pulkangka
nyinangi.
Palu
kutjungku
ngalinya
kuranu.
Nganalu
wanyu?
Papangku!
Munta
kutjupa
ngali
wantingu.
Ngananya
wanyu?
Ngaya.
Pula
pitjangu
wilu
wanara
kali
unngulta
tjiititingu.
Awari
pu:ntanu
ngura,
kali
mingkiri
kutjara
wiyari-
ngu.

We lived beneath
the ground, Warm
and snug
and round.
But one woe,
And that
Was
the cat!
To our joys
a clog,
In our
eyes a fog,
On our hearts
a log
Was
the dog!
When
the cat's
away,
Then
the mice
will play.
But,
alas!
one day;
(So
they
say)
Came
the dog
and cat,
Hunting
for
a bird,
Crushed
the mice
all flat,
Each one,
Where he lived
Underneath
the ground,
Warm
and snug
and round.
Think
of
that!

---

*This is Lewis Carroll's original hand-lettered manuscript version of the "Long Tale", slightly adapted; the version published in *Alice In Wonderland* was completely rewritten.

"Watarkun nyinanyi!" Mingkiringku Alitjila watjanu, "Nya: nyuntu kulini?" kuntangku watjanu Alitjilu, "Munta." Ka Mingkiringku watjanu, "Walykun alatjitu."

Ka Alitjilu alpamilantjikitjangku mapalku watjanu, "Walku? Ya:ltji awa? Pirukula wirulyaralku uru ilanytja. Wanyuna walku puta panangka tjutula." Munu paranyangangi.

Ka Mingkiringku pakara ankula watjanu, "Ngayunyan kurani alatji kawakawa wangkantjatjanungku."

Ka ngaltutjarangku Alitjilu ma-altira watjanu, "Munta, ngurpangkuna ngunti wangkangu, awari malaku pitja Mingkiri putitja. Mulapa nyuntu untju mulyararipai."

Palu Mingkiri mulyararira anu alatjitu.

Ka Alitjilu piruku ma-altingu, "Wanyu malaku pitjala tjukurpa wiyala."

Palu kata urira ma-tarararingu.

Ka ma-wiyaringkunyangka Luringku watjanu, "Ngaltutjara."

Ka Wanatjiti Minymangku watjanu untalta, "Ala palatja! Nyuntu puta palu purunypa mulyarariwiyangku wantima." Ka ngapartji watjanu wayiririra, "Pilunari Nguntju!"

Ka Alitjilu watjanu, "Awari utina putji ngayuku katima. Paluru mantu ma-mantjilpai. Mulapa paluru ayinayiningku mingkiri, tjulpu kulu witilpai munu mapalku ngalkupai.

Alatji wangkanyangka kuka tjulpu uwankara pulkara nguluringu, munuyanku wangkangi kaya tjara ankuntjikitja pakanu. Ka Kurparungku pakara watjanu, "Awa liri pikana puta mapalku ara ngurakutu." Ka Lu:npangku palumpa kulunypa tjuta ulkarurira altira watjanu, "Ngalya-pitjaya. Kuwari nyanga munga kulturingu, inkariringkala puta tjarpa."

"You are not attending!" said the Hopping Mouse to Alitji severely. "What are you thinking of?"

"I beg your pardon," said Alitji, very humbly. "It was just a slip."

And the Hopping Mouse replied: "Then you shouldn't be so slippery."

"Slippery," repeated Alitji, ready to make herself useful, and looking anxiously about her. "That's it! We'll slip into the claypan again; I'll sprinkle some earth over it."

"You insult me by talking such nonsense," said the Hopping Mouse, getting up and walking away.

"I'm so sorry," pleaded poor Alitji, "I didn't mean it. Do come back, Hopping Mouse dear, and finish your story. Really, you are so easily offended."

But the Hopping Mouse only shook his head and walked a little faster.

"Poor thing," remarked the Snake as the Hopping Mouse disappeared.

And an old Centipede said to her daughter, "There now, let that be an example to you not to have fits of the sulks." But young Centipede only answered cheekily, "Be quiet, Mother."

And Alitji said, "Well, I should have brought my cat. *She*'d have soon fetched the Hopping Mouse back. She's a great one for catching mice and birds, and she no sooner catches them than she eats them!"

This speech caused great fear among the birds, and they all began to talk at once, and some to move off. One old Magpie said, getting up, "I must go home, on account of my sore throat," while the Kingfisher called to her young in a trembling voice, "Come along, dears, it's growing dark and we must return to the river bank."

Kaya uwankara kutjupa kutjupa wangkara anu, ka Alitjinya lutju nyinangi.

"Munta, utina putji wangkawiyangku wantima. Uwankaraya palumpa kuraringkupai ngura nyangangka, palu mulapa paluru putji wiru alatjitu, awari putji putitja ya:larananta piruku nyakuku?"

Ka Alitjinya wangkara pulkara watjilarira piruku ulangu. Munu kuwaritu munmurpa ilaringkunyangka kulinu munu Mingkiri malaku pitjanyangka kulira pukultu ira-nyangu.

So, on various pretexts, they all moved off and Alitji was left alone.

"I wish I hadn't mentioned my cat; no one here likes to hear about her, but truly, she is the dearest of creatures.—Oh, Pussy, dear, when shall I see you again?"

Talking in this way made Alitji feel homesick once more and she began to cry. However, in a little while she heard footsteps approaching and looked up eagerly, thinking that the Hopping Mouse was returning.

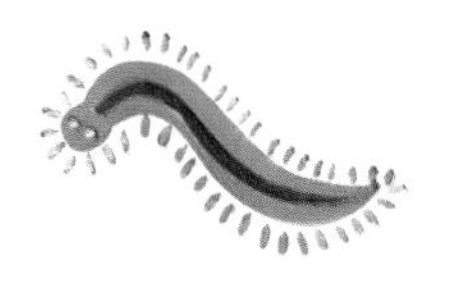

Malungku Tinka Witura Iyanu

Malu Piranpa tultjarukatira malaku pitjangi iluruilururira para-nyakula munu wangkarinangi: "Piriyitjanya, awari, Piriyitjanya. Ya:ltji panyatja? Awarinatju, tjitjantankukuni. Palu ya:ltjingkana punkatjinganu awa?"

Ka mapalku kulinu Alitjilu, "Muntauwa yakutja, kali kulu paluru ngurini," munu wanganarangku para-nguriningi, palu rawangku alatjitu putu ngurinu. Uwankara kunyu kutjuparingu—uru panya ilanypa, kulpikulpi ala panya utju tjutatjara, winki wiyaringu.

Ka Alitjilu para-ngurinyangka Malu Pirantu nyangu munu mirpantu mirara watjanu, "Untal nya:ringanyin nyangangka? Ngurakutu wala pulka wirtjapakala munutju yakutja mantjila, kali kulu, munu ngalya-kati. Wala pulka tjitjawa!" Ka Alitjinya nguluringkula mapalku wirtjapakanu kulira, "Ngayunya untalpa palku kulinu munu urulyaralku kuwari ngayunya ngurkanankula. Wanyuna puta yakutja palumpa ngurira mantjira kati."

Munu paluru wirkanu wiltja wirungka munu tjarpangulta kulira, "Nya:kuni witura iyani malungku?

The White Kangaroo sends in a Little Tinka

It was, however, the White Kangaroo hopping slowly back, looking anxiously about and saying, "The North Wind Spirit, oh dear, the North Wind Spirit! Where can they be? She'll have me executed. Where can I have dropped them?"

Alitji guessed in a moment: "Of course, he's looking for his dilly-bag and woomera!" and good-naturedly she began to hunt for them, but although she searched for some time she was unable to find them. Everything seemed changed. The pool of tears, the bats, the large cave with its narrow openings—all these had disappeared.

Soon the Kangaroo noticed Alitji as she hunted about and called to her angrily: "Daughter, what are you doing here? Run back to camp quickly and fetch my dilly-bag and woomera. Hurry, child!"

Alitji was so frightened that she ran off at once, thinking to herself, "He imagines I'm his daughter. How surprised he will be when he finds out who I really am. But all the same, I'd better take his dilly-bag to him."

She came to a well-made wurlie and went inside it, thinking, "Why is a Kangaroo ordering me about? My

Alitji tried to help the White Kangaroo find his woomera and dilly bag.

Alitjilu yakutja Malu Piranku nguriningi.

Putjingkulpintini kuwari witura iyalku kani tjinguru ngunytjungku altiku, kana ngapartji watjalku, ''Wiya Ngunytju putitja, putuna pitjanyi. Putjingkuni markunu mingkiriku ngura nyakuntjaku, mingkiri pakara ankuntjaku-tawara. Palu ngura ngayukungkaya putji pailpai anangu tjuta witunyangka.''

Ka kunyu wiltja palula tjuta utitjunu, yakutja panyatja kulu ngaringi, ka mantjira malakukutura nyangu tjuratja, ''Ngangari tjikilkuna—uliringuna.''

Munu arkanu tjukutjuku munu mapalku katangku pungu wiltja katutja. Munu rawatu pulkaringkuntjatjanu tultjungarakatingu munu piruku ngarikatingu munu kunyu nyi:ku kutju wiltja tja: wanu utiringu. Munu ngaltutjara tjitji paluru rawa pulkaringangi ka wiltja anganu alatjitu. Ka tjampungku ma-untura wiltja alanu munu mara uti ngarangi wiltjangka katu munu muti kuluntanu.

Mununku watjanu, ''Kuwari nya:ringkuku? Putu alatjituna pakani.'' Munu paluru watjilarira ngura waltja wirunmanangi. ''Mulapa ngayuku ngura wiru alatjitu. Panya nyara palulana palu purunypatu titutjara nyinangi kaniya mingkiringku, malungkutu witura iyaliangku wantingi. Utina malu panyatja wanaliyangku wantima. Palu nya:ringuna ngayulu awa? Utiya inma ngayunya inkama tjutangku inkara kulintjikitja. Pulkaringkulana ngayulunatju inma inkaku—munta, kuwaritu ngayulu pulkaringu awa, palu ya:lara ngayulu kungkawararingkuku? Mununa ya:ltjingara minymaringkuku wiltja nyanga utjungka ngarintjatjanu? Palya ngalulu pamparingkuwiya nyinama, mununa palyatu mai rungkaliya nyinama. Ya:ltjingarana mai rungkanma wiltja nyangangka, awa? Ngayulu kutjungku nyangatja angani alatjitu.''

cat will be telling me what to do next! Suppose my mother called me and I answered, 'No, Mother dear, I can't come. The Cat has told me to stay here and watch this mousehole in case the mouse escapes.' Only they'd send our cat away if she began ordering people about like that!''

Lots of things were hung up inside the wurlie and Alitji soon found the dilly-bag. She took it and was about to leave when she saw a wooden dish containing a cool, delicious drink which she knew was made from the flowers of a corkwood tree. ''Oh, I'm so thirsty, I'll drink it!'' she exclaimed.

She sipped a little of the drink, and immediately her head hit the top of the wurlie. Alas! She kept on growing and soon had to kneel down, and then to lie down. One elbow was pushed through the entrance and still she kept on growing, until the whole wurlie was choked and her left hand had pushed a hole in the roof and poked right through towards the sky. Her knees were pulled up to her chin.

''Now what will happen?'' Alitji thought. ''I simply can't get out.'' And she began to feel homesick again. ''How pleasant it was in my own country,'' she thought. ''I was always the same size there, and kangaroos and mice didn't order me about. I should never have followed the White Kangaroo in the first place. Whatever has happened to me? I should make a corroboree about myself so that people could sing it. I shall, when I've grown up. But then, I've already grown up. How will I get any older than I am now? And how, cramped in this wurlie, shall I ever become a woman? Well, I'm glad I'll never be an old woman and grind seed

Alitji filled the wurlie completely and was stuck.

Alitjinya pulkaringu ka wiltja anganu alatjitu.

Wangkara wangkara palurunku ngapartji wangkangi munu kulinu urilta katu wangkanyangka, "Untal! Untal! Nya:nin? Yakutjatju mapalku ngalya-kati!" Ka tultjarukatira ngarala watjanu, "Nyangatja nya:?" Nyi:ku tja:ngka ngarantja nyakula watjanu.

Ka wiltja unngu Alitjinya tjititingangi, ka wiltja winki tjititingangitu, palu ngunti paluru nguluringu, panya Malu tjuku nguwanpa ka paluru pulka ngurpatja.

Ka watjanu Malu Pirantu tja: wanu putu tjarpantjatjanungku, "Tatirana alara katu wanu tjarpaku." Munu tatiningi. Palu Alitjilu mara lipiringkula puta witira untunu, ka punkara waranmanu. Ka kulinu Alitjilu, "Muntauwa tjilkangkaltal punkanu." Munu kulinu mirpantu miranyangka, "Wayuta! Wayuta! Ya:ltjin?" Ka ngapartji watjanu, "Nyanga mangatana tjawani, Mayatja."

for food. Anyway, how could I grind flour in here? Simply by lying here, doing nothing, I fill this wurlie completely."

So Alitji went on making conversation with herself until she heard a loud voice calling outside.

"Daughter! Daughter! What are you doing? Bring my dilly-bag here at once." Then the voice said: "What's this?" Apparently the Kangaroo had seen Alitji's elbow, blocking the entrance to the wurlie.

Alitji began to tremble so that the whole wurlie shook. But there was no need for her to be afraid; she had grown so large that beside her the Kangaroo seemed quite small.

Unable to enter through the doorway because of Alitji's elbow, the Kangaroo said, "I shall jump up and get in through the roof." He began to clamber up, but Alitji suddenly spread out one hand and made a snatch. She heard a fall and a shriek and thought to herself, "He's fallen into some prickles"—and then she heard an angry shouting: "Possum, Possum, where are you?" And a reply: "Here, master. I'm digging for quandongs."

"Ngangkarku mangatan tjawani! Ngalya-pitja!" Pulkara mirpanaringu Malu Piranpa munu watjanu, "Nya: palatja wiltja katu ngaranyi?"
Ka watjanu Wayutangku, "Mi:na mantu."
Ka painu Malungku, "Kawakawan alatjitu. Nganalu mi:na pulka nyangu? Itara purunypa palatja."
Ka watjanu, "Uwa mantu, palu mi:nalta ngaranyitu."
Ka Malu Pirantu watjanu palula, "Ala mantjira ma-kati. Nya:ku paluru ngayuku ngurangka ngaranyi?"
Ka pilunaringu. Ka kuwaritu Alitjilu tjalymara wangkanyangka kulinu, "Ngayulu wantinyi, Mayatja, awa pulka palatja." "Ngangka! Mapalku ma-pitjala mantjila! Nguluringkupai mantu nyuntu."
Ka Alitjilu piruku mara lipiringkula puta witinu, munu waranmankunyangka kutjara kulinu. Munu pataningi palu uwankara pilunaringu.
Munu ngula mulapa kulinu tjuta ilaringkunyangka. Kaya kinkinmara yuruyuruningi, "Ya:ltji panyatja, awa?" "Ngalya-kati!" "Purkarangku ngana, katanankukun." "Nyuntu tatila!" "Wala, ma-tatilalta awa!" "Wiya ngayulu wantinyi!" "Ala tjungula." "Wiya, Ti:nka nyuntu tatila." "Tatila kunyu!" "Untulala, untula!" "Awa punkani, ngaltutjara." "Wanyula piruku untula." "Ala witilalta." "Alu, alu, tatinulta!" "Walangku tjanpi pala araltjara."

"Digging for quandongs, indeed! Come here!" said the Kangaroo impatiently. "What do you think this is, poking out of the top of the wurlie?"
"Sure, it's an arm," said the Possum.
"Stupid! Whoever saw an arm that size? It's as big as a river gum," said the Kangaroo.
"Yes, that's so, but it is an arm, for all that."
"Well, go and get it and take it away," said the Kangaroo.
"What's it doing in my wurlie?"
There was a silence for a while, and then Alitji could hear whispers: "I don't like it, it's so big."
"Coward, go and get it when I tell you."
At last she spread her fingers and made another snatch. This time she heard two shrieks and two thuds and waited, but there was only silence.
After a long time, Alitji heard the sound of many pattering feet approaching, and voices all talking together.
"Where is it?"
"Bring that over here."
"Go carefully there, you'll knock it down."
"You climb up."
"No, I don't want to."
"Altogether!"
"No, you climb up, Tinka."
"Go on, climb up!"
"All push, push!"
"Oh, he's falling, poor thing!"
"Push again."
"Hold on there."
"Oh, he's up!"
"Hurry now, pull on that spinifex!"

Ka Alitjilu unngu ngarira kuliningi munu pirintja kulinu wiltjangka katu munu muti kuluntankula pulkara makantunu; ka ngaltutjara, Ti:nka panya paluru makaturingu ilkaringka munu ngangkalingka mawiyaringkula piruku utiringkula punkaningi. Ka Malu Pirantu katungku watjanu, ''Ala witilaya!'' Ka witinu kutjupangku kantuntja alatjitu. Ka kulinu Alitjilu wiltja unngunguru kinkinmankunyangka. ''Ngaltutjara!'' ''Minaya mantjila.'' ''Warilaya!'' ''Ai pu:ntananyi nyura! Ma paturiwaya!'' ''Kata ampula awa!'' ''Palyaringanyin?'' ''Wanyulanya tjakultjura. Nya:ringu nyuntu?''

Ka tjalymara watjanu, ''Wampanti. Ngayulu watarku nyinangi kani pungu kutjupangku kana wu:luru purunypa ilkari wanu parpakanu.''

''Uwa mantun''—tjungungkuya urulyarara watjanu.

Ka Malu Pirantu watjanu, ''Wiltjala puta tilila.''

Ka Alitjilu katu mulatu mirara watjanu, ''Wiltja tilinyangkampa ngayulu putji ngayukungka iritjunkuku, nyuranya patjantjaku.''

Ka mapalku winki pilunaringu, ka kulinu Alitjilu, ''Utiya wiltja nyangatja araltjanama.''

All this Alitji heard from inside the wurlie, and then there was a scratching noise about the top of the wurlie. She drew up her knee and kicked upwards as hard as she could, then waited.

The first thing she heard was a general chorus, "There goes Tinka!"

"Hello, he's disappeared through the clouds."

"Here he comes."

And then she heard the White Kangaroo's voice alone: "Catch him, you there!"

Then silence, followed by a babble of voices.

"Poor thing!"

"Support his head."

"Fan him."

"Give him water."

"Here, you're smothering him, move back, all of you."

"Are you feeling better?"

"Tell us what happened."

"He's almost broken in two!"

At last a feeble voice answered, "I don't think I know. One minute I was up there and then something hit me and like a comet I flew across the sky."

"You certainly did," they all agreed with wonder.

"We must set fire to the wurlie," said the Kangaroo.

At this, Alitji called out very loudly, "If anyone sets fire to the wurlie I'll set my cat on you!"

Immediately, everyone was quiet and Alitji thought, "Why don't they take the wurlie to pieces?"

Left: *Tinka, the lizard lying back in the arms of two ant-lions.* Right: *A crowd of small birds watched Tinka recovering from his fall.*

Tjampu: *Tinka wawanpa ngaringi ka Lukupupu kutjarangku palunya ampuningi.* Waku: *Tjulpu kutjupakutjupa tjutangku ilaringkula Tinka ngaltutjara nyangangi.*

Munu kuwaritu pankalykatintja kulinu munu wangka kulinu, ''Tjungungkula.'' Ka punkapunkaningi puli tjukutjuku tjuta, munuya tjarangku Alitjinya mulya pungu ka mulyararira katu mirangu, ''Wanti!'' Ka piruku winki pilunaringu.

Ka puli tjuta punkara tjalaringu, ka nyakula urulyaranu munu uranu kulira, ''Tjinguruna ngalkuntjatjanu kutjupariku.'' Munu kutju tjalantankula ku:ltjunu, munu mapalku tjukutjukuringu.

Urilkutu wirtjapakara nyangu tjananya kaputurinyangka tjulpu tjukutjuku tjuta, kuka kutjupa kutjupa kulu, ka panya paluru Ti:nka ngaltutjara ngururpa wawanpa ngaringi ka Lukupupu kutjarangku ampura kanyiningi. Kaya uwankara Alitjinya utiringkunyangka pika pitjangu, palu Alitjinya ma-wirtjapakanu wala pulka munu tjatangka kumpinu.

Mununku watjanu, ''Piruku pulkaringkuntjikitjangkuna puta wararangku kulila munu palula malangka ngura panya wirukutu ankuntjikitjangku.''

Palu ya:ltjingara? Tjitji paluru iluruilururira para-nguriningi tjatangka, munu kunyu kulinu walkurkanyinyangka munu ira-nyakula papa kulunypa palunya walu-nyakunyangka nyangu. Ka papa paluru Alitjinya pampuntjikitja mara wararingu. Ka watjanu, Alitjilu, ''Ngaltutjara,'' munu utinmankula arkanu, palu ngulu mulatu putu nya:nu kulintjatjanungku, ''Paltjatjiratjangkuni kuwari winki ngalkuni.'' Munu punu tjukutjuku unytjungku mantjira ma-ilanu.

Ka papa mapalku tjina tjungu katuringkula wararakatingu, munu pukularira walkukanyira ngalya-mapalku-patjara wararatjinganingi. Ka Alitjinya tjirkara rangkirangkingka kumpira pupangu, ka kampa kutjupanguru nyirkinyangka papa piruku ngalya-

After a time she heard stealthy footsteps, then someone whispered, ''All together now,'' and a handful of small pebbles came raining down on her, some hitting her in the face. She shouted angrily, ''Stop that!'' and again there was silence.

Alitji noticed with some surprise that as the pebbles fell, they turned into honey-ants, and she picked one up, thinking, ''If I eat one, it's sure to change me.'' So, bursting one, she swallowed the sweet liquid—and began to shrink.

She ran out of the door, and saw quite a crowd of small birds and animals, and in the middle of them, the lizard they called Tinka was lying back in the arms of two ant-lions. They all made a rush towards Alitji when she appeared, but she ran off quickly and hid in a thick bush nearby.

''I'd better think first about how to grow back to my normal size,'' she thought, ''and then about how to get into that beautiful place I saw. But how am I going to change my size again?''

She wandered about among the trees, looking for something to eat. Then a sharp little bark made her glance up. An enormous Puppy was looking down at her, stretching out one paw to try to touch her.

''Poor little thing,'' said Alitji, and she tried to whistle to it, but she was so very frightened that she couldn't. ''If it's hungry,'' she thought, ''it will eat me whole.''

Hardly knowing what she did, she picked up a little stick and held it out to the Puppy, whereupon, with a yelp of delight, the Puppy jumped into the air, all four legs off the ground at once, rushed at the stick, and began to worry it. Alitji dodged behind a cassia bush to keep herself from being trampled on; the moment she wararakatira punkanu, punu panya tjukutjuku witintjikitja pulkara mukuringkula. Ka Alitjilu kulinu, "Awari nya:kuna pulka mulata inkanyi? Kuwarini kantura pu:ntankuku." Munu piruku rangkirangkingka kumpinu, palu papa watarkuriwiya tjalypa ngaurarara tjuta ara ma-paturingkula ngalya-wirtjapakaningi, munu ngula kutju pakuringkula patu nyinakatira ngangalymanangi tjalinpa uti, kuru pu:ringkulatu.

Ka pakuringkuntja nyakuntjatjanu Alitjinya pakara wala pulka wirtjapakara wirtjapakara nga:lpa watalpi wiyaringu munu ma-pararirira purkara walkurkanyinyangka kuliningi.

"Palu mulapa paluru papa kulunypa ngaltutjara, wiru alatjitu." Alatji Alitjilunku watjanu inuntjingka pupakatira paku wiyaringkuntjikitja mununku nyalpingka wariningi. "Awa tjukutjuku nyinantjakuna kuraringanyi. Utina kutjupa ngalkula—palu nya: wanyu?"

Inuntji tjuta, ukiri, likara kulu para-nyangangi, palu mai wiya ngarangi. Munu kunyu tjitji paluru piruku malakukutura nyangu punu iritjarangka, ngantja, kalta makungku katu nyinara mingkulpa nyultjaningi. Pilunpa paluru watarku nyinangi maku pulka.

appeared on the other side, the Puppy made another rush at the stick and fell head-over-heels in its hurry to get hold of it. Alitji thought, "Why am I playing with this enormous creature? Any moment I shall be trampled and squashed."

Then the Puppy began a series of short charges at the stick, running a very little way forward and a long way back, and barking hoarsely all the time, till at last it sat down, panting, a good way off, with its tongue hanging out of its mouth and its great eyes half-shut.

Seeing her opportunity to escape, Alitji jumped up and ran until she was quite tired and out of breath and could hear the Puppy's barking only faintly in the distance.

"And yet what a dear little Puppy it was," she thought as she rested against a wild flower's stalk and fanned herself with a leaf. "Goodness, I'm tired of being so small. I suppose I should find something to eat. But what?"

She looked all around at the wild flowers and the grass and bark, but there was nothing edible. Turning round and tipping her head back, she gazed into a tree with mistletoe berries in it, and there she saw a large witchety grub chewing mingkulpa, oblivious of her presence.

Makungku Wituntja

Makungku Alitjinya piluntu nyangangi ka Alitjilu palunya ngapartji nyangangi rawangku. Ka watjanu Makungku, mingkulpa pinangka tjunkula, "Ngananyan?"

Ka kuntangku watjanu, "Wampanti. Mungawinkina Alitjinya kunkuntjanu pakanu palu tjuta ara ngayulu kutjuparinyi."

"Kakari, tjukurpa kumpilpan wangkanyi. Wanyuni tjakultjura."

"Wiya, putuna tjakultjunanyi, ngayulunatju wiya nyinanyi."

Ka watjanu Makungku, "Putunanta kulini."

Ka watjanu tjitjingku, "Putuna utini. Ngayulu kulu nyangatja putu nguwanpa kulini. Kawalirinyi ngayulu tjuta ara kutjuparintjatjanu."

Ka watjanu, "Muntauwa."

Ka Alitjilu palula watjanu, "Kuwari nyuntu karpikarpira palulanguru parpakalku munu nyuntu tjinguru palunyatjanu kata kawaliriku."

Ka watjanu, "Wiya mantuna."

Ka Alitjilu tjiturutjiturarira watjanu, "Muntauwa, nyuntu wiya, palu ngayulu tjuta ara kutjuparira kata kawalirinyi."

Ka mirpantu watjanu,"Nyuntu! Palu nyuntu ngananya?"

Advice from a Witchety Grub

The Witchety Grub looked at Alitji in silence for some time, and she returned his stare. At last, putting his mingkulpa behind his ear, he said, "Who are you?"

Shyly Alitji replied, "I don't quite know. This morning when I got up I was Alitji, but I've been changed several times since then."

"You're talking in riddles! Explain yourself."

"But I can't," said Alitji. "You see, I'm not myself."

"I cannot understand you," said the Witchety Grub.

Alitji replied, "I can't make it clearer. I can scarcely understand it myself. I'm quite lost from changing so often."

"I see," said the Witchety Grub.

"Perhaps," Alitji said, "some day when you have turned into a chrysalis and after that into a moth, I should think you will feel a little queer, won't you?"

"Not a bit," said the Witchety Grub.

"Perhaps you're different," Alitji said sadly. "But my poor head is whirling because of all the changes."

"You!"said the Witchety Grub angrily,"who are you?"

Alitji felt irritated by this lack of understanding. "I think you should speak first," she said. "Who are *you*?"

"Why?" asked the Witchety Grub. But Alitji was tired of getting nowhere, and walked off.

Alitji gazed up into a tree and saw a large witchety grub.

Alitjilu iranyakula maku pulka nyangu punungka.

Ka Alitjinya kulu mirpanaringu Maku ngalturingkuwiya piruku tjapinyangka, munu watjanu, "Uti nyuntu wararangku wangka. *Nyuntu* ngananya awa?"

Ka watjanu, "Nya:kuna?" Ka mulyararira pinkurarira anu, Alitjinya.

Ka altira watjanu, "Malaku pitja. Kuwarinanta mulamulangku wangkaku."

Ka Alitjinya kulira malaku pitjangu.

Ka watjanu Makungku, "Mirpanariwiya nyinama." Ka Alitjilu pulkara palumpa kuraringkula watjanu, "Alatjitun wangkangu?"

Ka watjanu, "Wiya!"

Alitjinya patanu piruku wangkantjaku. Ka Makungku punu katu nyinara mingkulpa nyultjaningi watarkungku. Munu wangkawiya nyinara ngula kutju tjapinu, mingkulpa mantjira, "Mulapa nyuntu kutjuparingu?"

Ka watjanu, "Uwana. Kutjupa tjuta ngayulu putu kulini kuwari mununa wararingkula piruku tjukutjukuringkupai."

"Nya: tjuta nyuntu putu kulini?" Alatji Makungku tjapinu.

Ka tjiturutjituru mulatu watjanu Alitjilu, *"Ngintaka Kanpi Panyatja* ngayulu nguntingunti inkangi inma mulapa putu kulira. Awarinatju."

Ka watjanu Makungku, "Ala, inma inka, *Tjamu Nyuntu Tjilpiringu!"*

"Come back!" the Witchety Grub called after her. "I've something important to say to you."

Hearing this, Alitji came back.

"Keep your temper," said the Witchety Grub.

"Is that all?" said Alitji, swallowing her anger as well as she could.

"No," said the Witchety Grub.

Alitji waited for him to speak again. For some time he chewed on his mingkulpa just as though she were not there, but at last he put the mingkulpa behind his ear and asked, "Have you really changed?"

"Yes," said Alitji, "there are things I can't remember, and also, I keep altering my size."

"What are the things you can't remember?" asked the Witchety Grub.

Very sadly Alitji said, "I've tried to sing *Ilili nyampulnyampul*, but it all came out differently, and I can't remember what it should be. Oh, dear."

"Well, sing for me," said the Witchety Grub. "Sing *You are old, Grandfather*."

Ka Alitjilu tjapurpungkula inma inkangu:

Nyi:nkangku watjanu, "Nyuntu tjilpiringu
Munun kata nguru ngarapai.
Tjamu putitja, kura nyangatja
Utin tjilpingku wantima."

Ka watjanu, Tjamu tjilpingku
"Wiya palya mantuna
Kampa kutjuparira ngayulu
Katanguru ngarapai."

Nyi:nkangku watjanu, "Nyuntu tjilpiringu
Munun kanpi pulkaringu
Palu kampakutjupan tjarpangu;
Nya:ku wanyu tjamu?"

"Tjitjingkulpinatju tjunta
Kapulitjangka nyitinu
Munu anangu winki tjularingu
Utin palu purunymanama."

Nyi:nkangku watjanu, "Katiti wiyangku
Nyuntu kipara ngalkunu
Tarka nyalpi winkin ngalkunu;
Awa ya:ltjingaran wanyu?"

"Kurirarangkuli ngali
Tjakangku wangkara waningi,
Kana palunyatjanu kuwaritu
Tja: kunpu nyinanyi."

And Alitji began to sing, beating time on her thighs:

"You are old, Grandfather," the initiate said,
"And your hair has become very white;
And yet you incessantly stand on your head—
Do you think, at your age, it is right?"

"In my youth," Grandfather replied to this boy,
"I feared it might injure the brain;
But now that I'm perfectly sure I have none,
Why, I do it again and again."

"You are old," said the youth, "as I
mentioned before,
And have grown most uncommonly fat;
Yet you turned a back-somersault in at the door—
Pray, what is the reason of that?"

"In my youth," said the sage, taking three
big jumps,
"I kept all my limbs very supple
By the use of this kidney fat—kept in small lumps—
Allow me to give you a couple."

"You are old," said the youth, "and your jaws
are too weak
For anything tougher than suet;
Yet you finished the turkey with bones
and the beak—
Pray how did you manage to do it?"

Nyi:nkangku watjanu, "Tjamu mulyangkun
Nyuntu liru katunu;
Palu ya:ltjingaran awari
Nyuntu tjilpingku nya:nu?"

"Rawangkuni nyuntu tjapini
Kana karkararingu.
Ara, kuwarinanta kantuni,"
Munu paira iyanu.

Ka Makungku watjanu "Nguntin inkangu."

Ka watjanu kuntangku, "Munta, tjarana ngunti inkangu."

Ka watjanu, "Winki alatjitun ngunti inkangu."

Ka pilunpa ngarangi.

Ka ngula kutju Makungku watjanu, "Piruku pulkaringkuntjikitjan mukuringanyi?"

"In my youth," said Grandfather, "I laid down
the law,
And argued all day with my wife;
And the muscular strength which it gave to my jaw
Has lasted the rest of my life."

"You are old," said the youth, "one would
hardly suppose
That your eye was as steady as ever;
Yet you balanced a snake on the end of
your nose—
What made you so awfully clever?"

"I have answered three questions and
that is enough,"
Said Grandfather; "You make me quite tired!
Do you think I can listen all day to such stuff?
Be off, or I'll kick you outside!"

"That was all wrong," said the Witchety Grub.

"Some of it was right," said Alitji timidly.

"The whole thing was completely wrong," said the Witchety Grub, and there was silence.

After a time he spoke again. "Do you want to grow larger?"

"Yes," said Alitji doubtfully. "I want to be the same

"Uwanti. Ngayulu palu purunypa rawa nyinantjaku mukuringanyi, panya kampa kutjuparintja kura mulapa. Nyuntu kulu manti palumpa kuraringkupai."

Ka Makungku watjanu, "Ngalulu ngurpa alatjitu."

Alitjilu ngaparku wangkawiyangku wantingu, munu kunyu mirpanaringu Makungku rawangku tunguntunguntu wangkanyangka.

Ka piruku watjanu palula, "Palya nyuntu nyinanyi, mutu mulapa?"

"Wiya, pulkaringkuntjikitjana mukuringanyi, mutu mularku ngayulu kuraringanyi."

Ka mulyararira katuringkula watjanu Makungku, "Ngayulu mutu mulapa nyinanyi. Palya mantu mutumutu nyinantja."

Ka ngaltutjarangku Alitjilu watjanu, "Munta nguntina wangkangu, ngurpangku." Mununku kulinu, "Mapalkuya mulyararipai ngura nyangangka, wiyanguru."

Ka Makungku piruku mingkulpa nyultjanu.

Ka Alitjinya pilunpa patanu piruku wangkantjaku. Ka ngula kutju mingkulpa mantjira tja:katingu kutjara ara, mununku anangu winki urira watjanu, "Kampa kutjungku mutulpai, ka kampa kutjupangku waralpai."

Ka Alitjilunku kulinu, wangkawiyangku, "Nya:na kampa kutjupa ngalkuku?"

Ka katu palku wangkanyangka Makungku ngapartji watjanu, "Ngantja mantu."

Ka Alitjilu ngarala punu ngantjatjara nyangangi, kampa kutjara ngurkanankuntjikitjangku, munu wakungku ngantja alintjaratja mantjinu munu tjampungku ulpariratja mantjinu. Ka Maku punununguru ukalingkula ma-wiyaringu. Ka kunyu marangku kanyira putu pulanya ngurkanankula wakutja tjukutjuku katitingku patjanu. Ka mapalku ngutungunku tjina

size all the time. I don't like so many changes. You wouldn't like it, either."

"I wouldn't know," said the Witchety Grub.

Alitji said nothing; but she felt she was losing her temper as a result of being contradicted so much.

The Witchety Grub said: "Are you content now, to be very short?"

"No," said Alitji. "I don't like being very short. I would like to be taller."

Stretching himself up, the Witchety Grub said sulkily, "I am very short and consider it a good size to be."

"I beg your pardon," poor Alitji said, "I didn't mean it." And she thought to herself, "They are all so easily offended!"

He put the mingkulpa in his mouth again and began to chew it.

Alitji waited patiently until the Witchety Grub should speak again. At last he took the mingkulpa from his mouth, yawned twice, and said: "The berries on one side will make you grow shorter and those on the other side will make you grow taller."

"The other side of what?" Alitji thought to herself.

The Witchety Grub said: "Of the tree, of course," just as though she had spoken aloud.

Alitji looked at the tree with the mistletoe hanging from its branches, trying to decide which were the two different sides. At last she took a sprig of berries from the north side with her right hand, and a sprig from the south side with her left hand. Meanwhile, the Witchety Grub crawled down from the ironwood tree and disappeared. Alitji looked at the berries in either hand; unable to decide which was which, she nibbled a few from her right hand. Immediately, her chin hit her feet.

pungu, "Awarinatju wiyaringanyina," munu nguluringkula kampa kutjupitja mapalku ngalkuntjikitjangku arkanu palu ngutu tjinangka nyinantjatjanungku tja: putu nguwanpa alanu, palu tjukutjuku ku:ltjunu tjamputja.

* * *

"Ngangari katana piruku katuringu." Palu Alitjinya ngunti pukularingu. Alipiri paluru wiya ngarangi munu walu-nyakula liri wara ngurpatja kutju nyangu, ukiri pararitjanguru ngalya-pakanyangka.

Munu watjanu Alitjilu, "Nya: nyaratja tjaru mulapa iltinyi? Ka alipirimpa awa? Ka marampa? Ngaltutjara, nya:kunatju putu nyanganyi?" Alitjinya wangkara mara uringi palu putu nyangu, ka ukiri kutju tjaru mulapa uringi.

Ka tjitji paluru mara putu katuringkula kata pupakatingu munu liri tjula para-uringi. Munu tjaruringkula kata ukiri panyangka ilaringu, munu palunya nyalpi ngurkantanu, punu katu ngarantja, munu watalpi tjarpangu, palu ngalya-mapalku-parpakanu tjulpu aralapalpalpa, munu nyalpi pulkara urira Alitjinya mulya pungapungangi katu mirara, "Liru, liru!"

Ka watjanu, "Wiya alatjitu—ngayulu liru wiya. Wantimani."

Ka watjanu, "Pirukuna lirunmananyi," munu watjanu ula winkingku, "Awari putu alatjituna anga-kanyini."

Ka Alitjilu watjanu, "Nya: nyuntu wangkanyi? Ngayulu palumpa ngurpa alatjitu."

"Gracious, I'm disappearing!" she cried, and hastily she tried to take a mouthful from the left-hand sprig; but her chin was pressed so close against her foot that she could scarcely manage to open her mouth. However, she was able to swallow a few, from her left hand.

* * *

"Thank goodness my head is free," Alitji said happily. But her relief was short-lived. Her shoulders were nowhere to be found, and when she looked down, all she could see was an immense length of neck rising out of distant green leaves.

"What is all that green stuff?" she said. "And where are my shoulders? And my hands, poor dears, why is it I cannot see you?" Alitji was moving them as she spoke, but the only result seemed to be a shaking of the leaves.

Unable to bring her hands up to her head, Alitji tried bending her head down to her hands, and was delighted to find that her neck was flexible enough to move about in any direction. She curved it down to the green leaves, which she found to be nothing but the tops of trees, and was going to dive in among them when suddenly a pigeon flew at her, flapping its wings in her face and shrieking, "Snake, snake!"

"I'm not a snake," said Alitji indignantly. "Leave me alone."

"Snake, I say again!" the Pigeon said, and added with a sob: "I simply cannot keep them safe."

"I haven't the least idea what you are talking about," Alitji said.

A pigeon, guarding its nest, mistook Alitji's long neck for a snake.

Aralapalpaltu Alitjinya liri wara nyakula liru palku kulinu.

Ka Aralapalpaltu watjanu, "Tjanpingkana tjunu, inkariringka kulu, mununa piruku puntingka tjunu, palu liru, kakari liru!"

Ka Alitjilu putu alatjitu kulinu, munu wangkawiya patanu tjakultjunkuntjaku.

Ka rawangku tjiturutjiturungku wangkangi, "Ngampuna untjunmara kanyiningi mununa rawangku lirungka-tawara atunymanangi, mununa munga kutjupa munga kutjupa kunkunpa wiya alatjitu wanka nyinangi. Awarinatju."

Ka utiringu, munu Alitjilu watjanu, "Munta, mulapaya nyuntunya kuraningi. Ngaltutjara."

Ka rawangku wangkangi, "Ka punu nyangatja waintaringu kana manngu palyanu ka nyuntu mapalku ilkaringuru ngalya-ukalingu. Kakari liru!"

Ka pulkara watjanu, "Liru wiya mantu ngayulu, ngayuluna . . . ngayuluna . . . awari wampanti."

Ka watjanu, Aralapalpaltu, "Ala palatja! Nyuntu putu kulini. Mulapa nyuntu liru alatjitu."

Ka Alitjilu watjanu, "Tjitji kungka manti ngayulu."

Ka watjanu, "Nguntin wangkanyi. Ngayulu tjitji kungka mungilyi nyangu palu liri palu purunytjara wiya alatjitu. Nyuntu mantu liru ngaranyi. Wanyu nyuntu ngampu ngalkupai?"

Ka tjukarurungku watjanu, "Tjitji kungkangku tjulpu ngalkupai, kuka wiru."

Ka watjanu Tjulpungku, "Kakari, palurutu kutjara kura, kungka munu liru. Lirungku ngamputju ngalkupai ka tjitji kungkangku ngayunya."

"Munta. Mulapa ngananana kutjupa arangku kuka tjulpu ngalkupai, palu kuwari ngayulu nyuntunya wantinyi. Ngalkulana tjinguru piruku kampa kutjupariku."

"I've tried the spinifex and the banks of creeks, and the cassias, but the snakes—oh dear, the snakes!"

Alitji was more and more puzzled, but she waited for the Pigeon to explain.

The Pigeon went on dejectedly: "I've been keeping the eggs warm and constantly guarding against snakes and remaining alert night after night with no sleep—oh dear, oh dear."

Alitji began to understand. "I'm sorry you've been annoyed."

"And now," the Pigeon went on, "I've built my nest in the very highest tree, and straight away you come down from the sky. Ugh—snakes!"

"But I'm not a snake," Alitji said firmly, "I'm . . . I'm a . . . oh, I don't really know *what* I am."

"There," said the Pigeon. "You don't know that you are a snake."

"I think I'm a girl," Alitji said.

"You're lying. I have seen many little girls, but never one with a neck like that. You're a snake! Do you eat eggs?"

And Alitji answered honestly, "I eat the birds themselves—mmm, delicious meat!"

"Ugh," said the Pigeon, "they're all the same, girls and snakes. Girls eat birds, snakes eat birds' eggs."

"I'm so sorry," said Alitji. "Sometimes I do eat bird meat, but I really haven't come here to eat you. If I eat anything at all I'm likely to change size again, anyway."

"Well, be off, then," said the Pigeon, settling back sulkily on her nest.

Alitji crouched down among the trees as well as she could, for her neck kept getting twisted in the branches.

Ka mulyarangku watjanu, "Ala, ara!" munu manngungka nyinakatingu.

Alitjinya tjilinyinangu, palu liri kunyu punu parkangka karpikarpinu.

Munu kulinu "Muntauwa, nyangana kanyini marangku ngantja," munu arkanu kutjara munu wararingkula mutumuturingkula piruku wararingkula tjitji palya ngarangu munu pukularingu.

Munu palurunku wangkangi, "Alatjituna tjitji palyaringu, kuwarina puta ngura panya wirungka tjarpa. Palu ya:ltjipitinpa panyatja?"

Munu para-pitjala nyangu wiltja tjuku mulapa, munu kulinu, "Ngananya nyangangka nyinapai? Palu ngayukuya nguluringkuku anangu pulka nyakula." Munu ngantja wakungku kanyintja ngalkunu munu tjukutjukuringkula kutju wiltja kuluntja ilaringu.

Suddenly she thought: "Of course, here are the mistletoe berries still in my hand!" And she started to nibble at the left-hand and right-hand sprigs in turn, until, after growing alternately taller and shorter, she was just the right size.

She began to talk to herself, saying, "There now, I'm my usual self. The next thing is to find that lovely country. Now, in which direction would it be?"

As she wandered about, she came upon a very little wurlie. "Whoever lives here?" Alitji wondered. "They'll certainly be frightened if they see me this size." So she began nibbling at the right-hand berries until she grew small again, before approaching the wurlie.

Ninu Munu Itunypa

Alitjilu unytju nyinara patungku wiltja nyangangi, ka ngalya-mapalku-wirtjapakanu wati mulya antipina purunypa, munu warpungkula waru urara tilinu munu tjanpi mantjira tjunu ka tjunanpa pulka ilkaringka kirkitatjanu katuringu. Ka kunyu wiltja tja:ngka itingka wati kutjupa nyinangi mulya, ku[illegible]u kulu, nganngi purunypa. Ka Alitjilu pulanya mangka nyutirnyutirpa nyangu munu uwankara palya nyakuntjikitja ngalya-panykalkatira tjatanguru pakanu.

Ka Wati Antipinangku wararangku watjanu, "Kungkapa:ntuni wikaru iyani Piriyitjanya tjunanta altintjaku."

Ka ngaparku watjanu Wati Nganngingku, "Kungkapa:ntunta wikaru iyanu tjunanta altintjaku Piriyitjanya."

Ka pula pupakatingu warungka nyinakatintjikitja, mununku mangka tjunguringkula tjakaringu.

Alitjinya nyangaku pulkara ikaringu munu tjatangka piruku tjarpangu pula palunya kulintjaku-tawara. Munu piruku ma-nyirkira Mulya Nganngi kutju nyangu nyinara ilkari ira-nyakunyangka, kanti kutjupa anu.

Alitjilu wati kutjara nyangu warungka itingka nyinanyangka — kutju mulya antipina purunypa ka kutjupa mulya nganngi purunypa.

Bandicoot and Itunypa Root

As *Alitji stood* for a moment looking at the wurlie, a man with a face like a fish's suddenly came running from the bush. He collected some wood and hurriedly lit a fire, throwing spinifex on to it. Thick smoke rose towards the sky. Near the wurlie sat another man; his face and eyes were like those of a frog. Alitji noticed that they both had ochred hair, and in order to see everything properly, she crept a little way out of the bush.

The fish-faced man spoke first. "The Witch Spirit* has bade me send up a smoke-signal to call the Spirit of the North Wind to a corroboree."

The frog-faced man answered him: "The Spirit of the North Wind is called to a corroboree by a smoke-signal the Witch Spirit has bade you send up."

They both bent over to sit by the fire and their ochred curls became entangled.

Alitji laughed so much at this that she had to run back into the bush for fear of being heard. When she peeped out again, only the frog-faced man was in sight, sitting by the wurlie staring up into the sky; the other man, it seemed, had gone.

Alitji saw two men with ochred hair sitting beside a fire; one had a face like a fish and the other looked like a frog.

---

*Kungkapa:n translated here as "Witch Spirit", is the proper name of a certain malevolent female spirit who harbours evil intent towards young girls.

Ka wiltja tja:ngka waru ngarangi, ka palula minymangku mai pauningi, ka unngu pulkara kinkinmanangi, mirangitu, nyurtjingitu, ka kutjupa ara pulkara tu:lymanangi.

Ka Alitjilu pitjala ngulungulungku watjanu Mulya Nganngingka, "Palyana ma-tjarpa?"

Ka watjanu, "Ya:ltjingara? Waru pala angangaranyi, ka unngu nyuntu tjinguru pina patiringkuku—kulila, pulkaraya miranyi."

"Palu nyakuntjikitjana mukuringanyi."

Ka watjanu Mulya Nganngingku, "Nyangangkana mungawinki kitja nyinaku." Ka wiltjanguru ngalya-waningu pingkila, ka nguwanpa palunya mulya pungkula punu munkaritjangka punkanu. Ka rawangku wangkangi Mulya Nganngingku, watarkungku, "mununa piruku mungaringkuntjaku, tjinguru." Ka Alitjilu piruku watjanu, "Palu ya:ltjingara ngayulu ma-tjarpaku?"

"Tjarpawiya manti nyinama."

Ka watjanu tjalymarangku Alitjilu, "Uwankarangkuya tjakangku wangkara wanipai, ngura nyangangka. Kura alatjitu."

Ka rawangku panyangku wangkangi, "Ngayulu tjirirpi kutjupa tjirirpi kutjupa nyangangka nyinaku."

Ka Alitjilu watjanu, "Palu ngayulumpa?"

Ka watjanu, "Wampanti", munu utinmanangi.

Ka Alitjilu watjanu, "Karangki alatjitu paluru," munu waru wanu wararakatira wiltjangka tjarpangu.

Unngu tjunanpa pulka ngarangi, ka Piriyitjalu iti ampura kanyiningi, ka minyma panyangku mai

Near the entrance to the wurlie, a woman was cooking at a fire, while from inside came shouting and sneezing noises, and every now and then, a great crash.

Timidly Alitji approached the frog-faced man and said, "May I go inside?"

"How?" he said. "There's a fire in the doorway, and anyway, listen to that howling. You'll be deafened if you go in there."

"But I should like to see inside."

"I'm going to sit here until morning," Frog-face said; and at that moment a billy-can hurtled from the wurlie, narrowly missing his nose and landing under a tree beyond him. "Perhaps until nightfall," he added, as though nothing had happened.

"How can I get inside?" Alitji asked.

But Frog-face only said, "I shall sit here every day."

"But what about me?" Alitji said.

"I don't know," he replied, and started to whistle.

"He's perfectly idiotic," Alitji thought; and she stepped around the fire and went into the wurlie.

It was full of smoke. The Spirit of the North Wind was nursing a baby and the other woman in the wurlie was cooking itunypa roots. The whole place smelt of it, and they were all sneezing—except a Wild Cat, which was lying by the fire grinning.

"Why is she cooking so much itunypa root? There's far too much of it," Alitji thought. And then she said timidly, "Would you please tell me why your cat grins like that?"

Inside the wurlie the Spirit of the North Wind was nursing a baby, while another woman was cooking itunypa roots. A wild cat lay by the fire, grinning.

Wiltja unngu Piriyitjalu iti kanyiningi, ka minyma kutjupangku mai itunypa pauningi. Ka Ngaya warungka itingka ngarira ikaringangi.

pauningi—mai itunypa pauningi ka pulkara pantingi, kaya uwankara nyurtingi palu ngaya kutju wiya. Ngaya warungka itingka ngarira ikaringangi. Ka iti pinkara ulangi munu atjanmara nyurtingi.

Ka Alitjilunku nyurtira watjanu, "Nya:ku paluru itunypa pulka pauni? Uti wantima."

Alitjilu kuntangku watjanu tjanala, "Ngaya wanyu nya:ku ikaringanyi?"

Ka Piriyitjalu watjanu, "Tjaka mantu. Ngaya palatja ikaringkupai. Ninu!" Ini nyanga malatja katu mulapa watjanu, ka Alitjinya urulyarara tjirkanu, palu Piriyitjalu itingka wangkangu—Alitjila wiyangka.

Ka Alitjilu piruku watjanu, "Palu ngaya putu ikaringkupai."

Ka Piriyitjalu watjanu, "Ngaya mantu tjaka ikaringkupai. Nyuntu tjitji ngurpa alatjitu."

Ka watjanu, "Munta" munu pilunaringu kuntaringkula, kaya uwankara pilunpa nyinangi ka minyma panya mai paulpaingku tjuta mantjira iti, Piriyitjanya kulu atuningi. Mai panya ituntja, punungka, apungka, waya tjarangka, punu tja:tjarangka, uwankarangka pulanya atuningi. Ka Piriyitjanya watarku nyinangi pungkunyangkatu, ka iti rawa ulangi, panya kuwaripatjara paluru ulangi.

Ka nguluringkula pakara watjanu Alitjilu, "Awa ngaltutjara, wanti! Awa ngutun watalpi wiyanu punu pulkangka. Ngaltutjara, wanti!"

"Just habit," said the Spirit of the North Wind. "It always grins like that. *Bandicoot!*" She spoke the last word with such sudden violence that Alitji jumped with surprise; but the Spirit of the North Wind was speaking to the baby, not to Alitji.

Alitji spoke again. "But cats can't grin."

"They can," said the Spirit of the North Wind. "They all can. They grin all the time. Really, you know nothing."

"I beg your pardon," said Alitji humbly, and there was no more talking for a time; but then the woman doing the cooking started picking up everything within reach and throwing it at the baby and the Spirit of the North Wind: itunypa, firesticks, stones, billy-cans. The Spirit of the North Wind took no notice even when some of these things hit her. The baby just kept on howling—it had been howling all the time, anyway.

Much alarmed, Alitji jumped up, saying: "Oh, the poor little thing, you've almost knocked off his nose with that piece of wood. The poor thing, stop it!"

Ka watjanu palula Piriyitjalu, "Pilunari. Nyuntu ngananyan? Nya:kunin paini? Nyuntu tjitji malikitja alatjitu."

Ka nguwanpa ulara watjanu Alitjilu, "Ngaltutjara awa, kata."

Ka Piriyitjalu watjanu, "Uwa Katala."

Ka tjapinu Alitjilu, "Nya: katala?"

Ka watjanu, "Kata mantu katala."

Ka ngulungku malakukutura minyma mai paulpai nyangangi palu kulilwiyangku paluru mai rungkaningi. Ka Piriyitjalu iti pulkara uritjingara inma palula inkangu, alatji:

Kupikupi nyanga ngaranyi
Kala kinkinmananyi
Munula kawakawangku
Tja:tjarangka inkanyi.

Ka itingku mai paulpaingku kulukulu tjungungku palula inkangu—

Atja! Atja! atja! atja! atja! . . .

Ka iti katu wanira piruku witira kampa kutjupa inkangu. Ka iti katu mulapa ulanyangka Alitjilu inma putu nguwanpa kulinu.

Iti kuru alaringu
Nyurtjinyi, miranyitu
Kata tiwilarinyilta,
Pulkarana pungkuku.

Atja! Atja! atja! atja! atja . . .

But the Spirit of the North Wind only said: "Be quiet. Who are you to rebuke us? You are only a stranger."

Almost in tears, Alitji exclaimed, "Oh dear, his poor head."

"Yes," cried the Spirit of the North Wind, "chop it off!"

"Chop what off?" said Alitji.

"Chop off his head, of course!"

Fearfully Alitji turned round to look at the other woman, but she was so busy cooking that she seemed not to hear. Then the Spirit of the North Wind began to sing to the baby, shaking it about as she did so:

There's a whirlwind in this wurlie,
All is shouts and bangs and noise,
Everyone is crazed and surly,
Stones and firesticks are their toys.

Then the baby and the woman joined in the chorus:

Wow wow wow . . .

As the Spirit of the North Wind sang the second verse of the song, she kept tossing the baby violently up and down, and the poor little thing howled so that Alitji could hardly hear the words:

Little howler's eyes are staring,
Screams and sneezes fill the air,
Little head is quickly jerking,
I had better clout him there.

Wow wow wow . . .

Ka Piriyitjalu iti Alitjila wanira watjanu, "I:ku ngana. Ananyina Kungkapa:nta inkantjikitja."

Munu ma-pakanu, ka minyma mai paulpaingku ma-waningu punu tja:tjara palu puta atunu, wu:lukatinyangka.

Ka Alitjilu iti watalpi punkatjingara witira kulinu, "Mi:na, tjalpa tiwilpa nyangatja, kana putu nguwantu ampuni."

Ka iti rawa ngurmanangi munu tjuta ara nyutinyutiringkula tiwilaringi, ka putu nguwantu kanyiningi Alitjilu. Munu kalikalira pina waku, tjina tjampu witira urilkutu katingu kulira, "Wantikatinyangkampaya kunakululku." Ka iti ngapartji ngurmanu. Panya nyurtjintja wiyaringu.

Ka watjanu, "Ngurmankuwiyangku wantima. Wiru wiya palatja."

Ka piruku ngurmanu, ka Alitjilu iluruilurungku mulya palunya pulkara nyangu, pikatjara palku kulira, munu palunya mulya wara nyangu, munu kuru kulu nyangu utjuringkunyangka. Munu kulinu, "Iti nyangatja nya:ringanyi? Munta, ulanyi tjinguru," munu kuru nyangu, palu wiya, ilanypa wiya ngarangi. Munu palula watjanu Alitjilu, "Ninurinyangkampananta wantiku."

Throwing the baby to Alitji, the Spirit of the North Wind said, "Take it, you. I am going to a game with the Witch."

As she went out, the other woman threw a burning stick after her, but it missed.

Alitji caught the baby with some difficulty, thinking, "Its arms and legs are held out so stiffly I can hardly hold it."

The poor little thing was grunting and kept doubling itself up, then straightening itself out again, so that Alitji had great difficulty in keeping it in her arms. She twisted it up, and, with a tight hold of its right ear and left foot, carried it outside, thinking: "If I leave it here they are sure to kill it." To which the baby grunted in reply. (It had left off sneezing by this time.)

"Don't grunt," said Alitji. "It's not at all proper."

It grunted again, and Alitji looked anxiously into its face, thinking it must be sick. Certainly it had a very long nose and she noticed that its eyes were becoming extremely small. "What's happening to this baby?" she wondered. "Perhaps it is only sobbing." She looked into its eyes again, but there were no tears. "If you turn into a bandicoot," she said, "as I strongly suspect you are, then I shall have nothing more to do with you."

Ka ngaltutjara piruku ngurmanu, munta ulangu, wampa, ka pula wangkawiya anangi. Ka kuliningi Alitjilu, ''Nya:lkuna nyanga palunya ngura waltjangka wirkara?'' Ka katu ngurmanu, ka Alitjilu walu-nyakula palunya ninu alatjitu papulanu.

Alitjilu panangka ngaratjunu, ka palya alatjitu ma wirtjapakanu. Kanku watjanu, ''Pulkaringkula paluru tjitji kura nyinaku, palu ninu wiru, ngaltutjara.'' Munu Alitjilu tjitji kutjupa tjuta kulinu mununku watjanu, ''Kutjupa tjarantiya palya ninuriwa, palu ya:ltingarana tjananya kutjupanama?''

Munu ira-nyakula Ngaya panyatja witjinti mi:nangka katu nyinanyangka nyangu, munu urulyaranu.

Ka Ngaya ikaringu Alitjiku, ka palunya wanganara kulinu, palu milytji waraku, katiti tjutaku nguluringkula patu ngarala wangkangi, ''Ngaya ya: ltjipitinpana puta ara nyanganguru?''

Ka watjanu, ''Ya:ltjikutu ankuntjikitjan mukuringanyi?''

''Wampanti.''

Ka watjanu Ngayangku, ''Ala palatja! Mukuringkula ara.''

''Palu ya:ltjingkana wirkankuku?''

The poor thing grunted again, or perhaps it sobbed, it was hard to say which, and they went along without speaking. ''What shall I do with this creature when I get home?'' Alitji thought to herself. Suddenly it grunted very loudly indeed, and looking down, Alitji saw that it was indeed a bandicoot.

She set the little thing down and watched it trot happily away. ''If it had grown up it would have been a very ugly child,'' she said to herself, ''but it's a nice little bandicoot.'' She began thinking of some other children that she knew. ''Some of them might do very well as bandicoots,'' she said to herself. ''But how to change them, that's the thing?''

Looking up, she was startled to see the Wild Cat, sitting on the branch of a corkwood tree.

It was grinning down at her and she thought it seemed good-natured, but its claws were very long and it had a great many teeth, so she prudently kept her distance, and said, ''Cat, which way ought I to go from here?''

''It depends where you want to get to,'' the Wild Cat answered.

''I don't think I know,'' Alitji said.

''Well then, go whichever way you like.''

''But where would I arrive?'' Alitji asked.

Ka Ngayangku watjanu, "Wampa. Palu rawa ankulampan wirkankuku alatjitu."

Ka watjanu Alitjilu, "Mulamulangkun wangkangu." Munu tjapinu palula, "Anangu ngananya tjana ngura nyangangka nyinanyi?"

Ka wilitjunkula watjanu, "Palangka nyantju ka palangka wati puluka kanyilpai; kutjara pula kata kawakawa."

Ka watjanu, "Kawakawa wantipai ngayulu." Ka watjanu, "Uwankarala kata kawakawa ngura nyangangka, ngayulu kulu, nyuntu kulukulu."

Ka watjanu, "Nya:kun ngayunya kawakawanmananyi?"

Ka Ngayangku watjanu, "Kawakawa tjuta kutju ngura nyangakutu pitjapai."

Ka watjanu, "Ka nyuntunku nya:ku kawakawanmananyi?"

Ka watjanu, "Kulila, tjitutja tjuta wanyu kawakawa?"

"Wiya mantu."

Ka watjanu, "Tjitutja pukularira wipu uripai munu mirpanarira ngaurnmankupai. Palu ngayulu pukularira tjuni ngaurnmankupai mununa mirpanarira wipu uripai. Alatjituna kawakawa." Munu piruku watjanu, "Nyuntu kuwari inma inkaku Kungapa:nta?"

Ka Alitjilu watjanu, "Uwa ngayulu mukuringanyi, palu ngayunyaya altiwiyangku wantingu."

Ka watjanu Ngayangku, "Ngayunyalta nyakuku," munu arkayiringu.

Ka Alitjinya urulyaralwiya nyinangu. Panya ngura palula paluru tjaka urulyaraningi.

Ka piruku utiringkula watjanu, "Munta, itimpa?"

"I don't know," said the Wild Cat. "But if you went on for long enough you'd be sure to arrive somewhere."

"That's true," said Alitji. Then she asked, "Who lives around here?"

Pointing into the distance, the Wild Cat said: "Over there lives a Horse, and over that way a Stockman. They're both mad."

"I don't want to go among mad people," Alitji remarked.

"We're all mad here," said the Wild Cat. "I'm mad and you are, too."

"How do you know I'm mad?" asked Alitji.

"Only mad people come here."

"Well, why do you call yourself mad?" Alitji asked.

"Listen," said the Wild Cat. "Is a dog mad?"

"Certainly not," said Alitji.

"Well, when a dog is pleased it wags its tail and when it's angry it growls. But when I growl I'm pleased, and when I wag my tail I'm angry. Therefore, I'm mad." And then he asked, "Are you going to the Witch's game?"

"I should like to, but I haven't been invited," said Alitji.

"You'll see me there," said the Wild Cat, and vanished.

Alitji was not much surprised at this. She was getting well used to queer things happening. Appearing again, the Wild Cat said, "Bye-the-bye, what became of the baby?"

"It turned into a bandicoot," said Alitji, quite unperturbed.

Looking up, Alitji was startled to see the Wild Cat sitting on the branch of a corkwood tree.

Iranyakula Ngaya panyatja witjinti mi:nangka katu nyinanyangka nyangu Alitjilu, munu urulyaranu.

Ka ngapartji urulyaralwiyangku watjanu, "Ninuringu."

Ka wajanu, "Muntauwa, kulinuna," munu piruku arkayiringu.

Ka Alitjinya patanu piruku utiringkuntjaku, palu wiya, wiyaringu alatjitu paluru, ka Alitjinya ma-pitjangi puluka kanyilpaiku ngurakutu, mununku watjarinangi, "Nyanytju tjutana nganmantju nyangu, palu wati puluka kanyilpaiku ngurpa ngayulu.

Munu wangkara ira-nyakula Ngaya piruku nyangu urtjantja nyinanyangka.

Ka watjanu, "Ninuringu, munta mi:nuringu?"

Ka watjanu, "Ninuringu. Kulila, arkayirira mapalku utiringkuwiyangku wantima. Kata ngayulu urinyi."

Ka watjanu, "Munta," munu purkara arkayiringu, wipu nginti-nguru tjana wanu ikaringkuntja kutu, ka anangu winki wiyaringkunyangka ikaringkuntja kutju tjukutjuku ngarala wayaringutu.

Ka kulinu Alitjilu, "Ngaya ikaringkuntja wiya ngayulu nganmantju nyangangi, palu ikaringkuntja ngaya wiya, ngayulu kuwari kutju nyanganyi."

Munu ma-pitjala ma-pitjala wati panyaku ngura nyangu, munu palunya pulka nyakula ngantja tjamputja ngalkunu tjukutjuku wararingkuntjikitjangku, munu ngulungulu ma-ilaringu, kulira "Awari kawakawa alatjitu manti paluru. Utina Nyanytjuku ngurakutu anama."

"I thought it would," said the Wild Cat, and vanished again.

Alitji waited in case it returned, but no, it had gone for good, so she set off towards the Stockman's camp, saying to herself as she went along, "I've seen horses before, but never a stockman."

As she said this, she looked up and there was the Wild Cat again, sitting on a branch of a tecoma bush.

"Did you say 'bandicoot' or 'initiate'?" asked the Cat.

"I said bandicoot," said Alitji, "and listen—I wish you wouldn't keep on appearing and disappearing so suddenly. I'm becoming quite giddy."

"I'm sorry," said the Wild Cat, and this time it vanished quite slowly, starting at the tail and ending with the grin, which remained for some time after the rest of it had gone.

"I've often seen cats without grins," thought Alitji, "but this is the first time I've seen a grin without a cat."

She walked on, and soon saw the Stockman's camp. It all looked so large that she nibbled a few of the left-hand mistletoe berries to grow a bit taller, and then she approached timidly, thinking, "Oh dear, suppose he is quite mad? Perhaps I should have gone to visit the Horse instead."

The Wild Cat vanished into thin air.

Ngaya arkayirira wiyaringu.

Tjapa Ngalkuntja

A*litjilu ilaringkula* waru nyangu, ka nyinara tjikiningi Nyanytjungku pula Tjakumunungku. Ka ngururpa kuwala kunkunpa nyinangi, ka pula nyiku palula tjunkula kata wanu wangkangi.

Ka kulinu Alitjilunku, "Ngaltutjara, munta palya—paluru watarku kunkunarinyi". Munu Alitjinya ilaringkunyangka pula katu watjanu, "Anganu! Anganu!"

Ka watjanu, "Ngura nyangatja lipi mulapa," munu warungka itingka nyinakatingu.

Ka Tjakumunungku watjanu, "Kukakun mukuringanyi?"

Ka para-nyakula ti: kutju nyangu munu watjanu, "Kukana putu nyanganyi."

Ka watjanu, "Wiya ngaranyi."

Ka mirpanarira watjanu, "Kurangkunin ngalkuntjaku watjanu."

Ka Tjakumunungku ngapartji watjanu, "Ka nyuntu kura tjunguringkula nyinanyi, ngali altiwiyangku wantinyangka."

Ka watjanu, "Nyupalimpa kutju nyangatja? Waru nyanga pulka ngaranyi, wayatjara pulka kulu, ti: pulkatjara."

Ka Nyanytjungku rawangku Alitjinya

Billy Tea and Damper

D*rawing nearer* Alitji saw a fire, and both the Horse and Stockman were sitting beside it, drinking tea. Between them was a koala, fast asleep, and they were holding a conversation across its head, resting their elbows on it.

"Poor thing," thought Alitji, "but then I daresay it doesn't mind, as it's asleep."

As she drew near the fire, the Horse and the Stockman cried out, "No room, no room!"

"There is plenty of space," cried Alitji, and sat down by the fire.

"Have some meat if you'd like it," said the Stockman.

Alitji looked around. "I don't see any meat," she said.

"There isn't any," he said.

"Then it wasn't very civil of you to offer it," said Alitji angrily.

"And it wasn't very civil of you to sit down without being invited."

"Is it all for you?" she said. "This is a large fire and that is a large billy-can full of tea."

The Horse had been looking at Alitji for a long time.

The Horse and the Stockman were drinking tea around a fire, and resting their elbows on a koala who was fast asleep between them.

Nyantjungku pula Tjakumunungku warungka nyinara ti: tjikiningi, ka ngururpa Kuwala kunkunpa ngaringi.

nyakuntjatjanungku watjanu, ''Miri maru nyuntu. Utinku paltjila.''

Ka watjanu, ''Paltjiratu ngayulu maru nyinapai.''

Ka kulira Nyantjungku kuru pulkara alara watjanu, ''Ka:nka wanyu nya:ku tangka purunypa nyinanyi?''

Ka Alitjinya pukularingu kulira, ''Ngangari kuwarila ngalpangalpa wangkanyi,'' munu katu watjanu, ''Ninti ngayulu palumpa.''

Ka watjanu Tjakumunungku, ''Nyuntu palunya kulini mulapa?''

Ka watjanu, ''Uwana.''

Ka Tjakumunungku watjanu,''Utin wangkara kulinma.''

Ka Alitjilu watjanu, ''Tjakangku mantu ngayulu wangkara kulilpai, munta, kulira wangkapai ngayulu, ka palatja palu purunypa.''

Ka Nyantjungku watjanu, ''Wiya alatjitu, palu purunypa wiya. Wanyu palya ngayulu alatji wangkanyi, 'ngayulu nyakula ngalkupai,' munu piruku palu purunypatu, 'ngayulu ngalkula nyakupai'?''

Ka Tjakumunungku watjanu, ''Ka ngayulu alatji wangkanyi 'Ngayulu mantjira mukuringkupai,' munu piruku palu purunypatu, 'Ngayulu mukuringkula mantjilpai'?''

Ka Kuwalangku kunkunpa winkingku watjanu, ''Ka ngayulu wanyu alatji watjalku, 'ngayulu kunkunarira nga:kampapai' munu piruku palu purunypatu 'ngayulu nga:kampara kunkunaripai'.''

Ka watjanu Tjakumunungku, ''Uwa mantu palu purunpa alatjitu. Nyuntu mulapa nga:kampara kunkunaripai.''

Now he said: "Your skin is very dark. You ought to wash yourself."

"My skin is always dark, even after washing," Alitji replied with dignity.

The Horse opened his eyes very wide on hearing this, but all he said was, "Why is a crow like a tank?"

"Now we're going to have some fun," Alitji thought happily. "I know the answer," she said aloud.

"You mean you have thought it out?" said the Stockman.

"Yes," she said.

"You should think what you say," said the Stockman.

"I do think what I say—I mean, say what I think. It's the same thing," said Alitji.

"Not a bit the same," said the Horse. "You might just as well say that 'I see what I eat' is the same as 'I eat what I see'."

And the Stockman added, "You might just as well say 'I like what I get' is the same as 'I get what I like'."

"You might just as well say," said the Koala sleepily, "that 'I breathe when I sleep' is the same thing as 'I sleep when I breathe'."

"It *is* the same thing with you," said the Stockman. And they were all silent, while Alitji thought over the crow and the tank.

The Horse picked up the Stockman's rifle and said, "Really, this is useless. Why did you tell me to put salt in it?"

Rather embarrassed, the Stockman answered, "It was good salt."

Left: *The Koala — asleep again.* Right: *The Horse examined the Stockman's rifle.*

Tjampu: *Kuwala piruku kunkunaringu.*
Waku: *Nyanytjungku Tjakumunuku raipula nyangangi.*

Kaya uwankara pilunaringu, ka Alitjilunku ka:nka, tangka kulu pulkara kuliningi.

Ka Nyantjungku watjanu, raipula mantjira, "Ngangka:! Kuraringu nyangatja. Nya:kunin tjaltu tjarpatjunkuntjaku witunu?"

Ka kuntaringkula watjanu Tjakumunungku, "Munta. Tjaltu wiru panyatja."

Ka mulyararira watjanu, "Uwa mantu, palu purkutjara. Nya:ku tjaltu punu tja:tjarangka tjunu?"

Ka Tjakumunungku tjiturutjitururira raipula mantjira ti: tjutinu palula munu piruku watjanu, "Mulapa panyatja tjaltu wiru."

"Maybe," the Horse grumbled, "but it has ashes in it. Why did you push in the salt with a burnt stick?"

Gloomily the Stockman took the rifle and, pouring tea down the barrel, said: "It really was the best salt."

Alitji had been looking curiously at the rifle for some time, and now she said: "That rifle wouldn't shoot, it would only spear things."

"Naturally," said the Horse. "Would you shoot things with a woomera?"

"No," said Alitji, "we spear animals with a spear."

"Well then," said the Horse.

Poor Alitji simply could not follow the conversation at all, and after a while she said timidly, "I'm sorry, but I don't understand what you mean."

"The Koala is asleep again," said the Horse; and he poured some hot tea on to its nose.

The Koala shook its head and said, without opening its eyes, "Of course, of course. I agree entirely."

Ka kunyu Alitjinya raipula rawangku nyakula urulyaranu, munu watjanu, ''Raipula nyangatja wakalpai kutju, paulpaiwiya.''

Ka watjanu Nyantjungku, ''Uwa mantu. Nyura wanyu mirungka paulpai kuka?'' Ka watjanu, ''Wiya, nganana kulatangka wakalpai.''

Ka watjanu, ''Ala palatja!'' Ka Alitjilu ngaltutjarangku putu alatjitu kulira purkarangku watjanu, ''Munta. Putu nguwanpananta kulini.''

Ka watjanu Nyantjungku, ''Kuwala piruku kunkunaringu,'' munu ti: waru tjutinu mulyangka.

Ka Kuwalangku kata urira kuru patingku watjanu, ''Uwa mulapa, mulapa. Ngayulu kulu palunya kulini.''

Ka Nyantjungku Alitjinya para-nyakula watjanu, ''Panyatjan kulinu—ka:nka panya?''

Ka watjanu ''Wiya, putuna kulini. Wanyuni tjakultjura.''

Ka watjanu Nyantjungku, ''Ngurpa ngayulu.'' Ka Tjakumunungku watjanu, ''Ngayulu kulu.''

Ka pakuringkula watjanu Alitjilu, ''Rawangku nyupali kawakawa alatjitu wangkanyi ka nyanga tjintu tjarpanyi.''

Ka watjanu, ''Tjarpawiya ngaranyi paluru.''

Ka Alitjilu watjanu, ''Putunanta kulini. Ngurpa ngayulu palumpa.''

Ka watjanu Nyantjungku, ''Uwa mantu nyuntu Tjintuku ngurpa alatjitu.''

''Have you guessed the riddle yet?'' said the Stockman to Alitji.

''No. What's the answer?'' she asked.

''I haven't the slightest idea,'' said the Horse.

''Nor I,'' said the Stockman.

Tired of all this, Alitji said, ''You two have talked nonsense for so long that now the sun is setting.''

''It is not setting,'' said the Stockman, ''it is staying right where it is.''

''I can't understand you,'' said Alitji. ''I am very ignorant.''

''Yes,'' said the Horse, ''you are. You know nothing about the sun.''

''Perhaps,'' said Alitji, ''but I do stab tjintjulu* berries with my hair.''

''That accounts for it,'' said the Stockman. ''The sun won't stand piercing. But if you keep on good terms with him, he'll do anything for you. Listen! On Sundays the Sun and I are great friends. If I get up in the morning and don't feel like rounding up cattle, he immediately sets and there it is—supper time!''

''But then,'' said Alitji thoughtfully, ''you wouldn't be very hungry for it.''

*Tjintu, a similar-sounding word, means ''sun''. Alitji had decorated her hair with berries by twining a strand of hair around a small stick, at the same time piercing a berry with the stick.

Ka watjanu Alitjilu, "Uwanti. Palu wakalpai ngayulu tjintjulu, mangkangka."

Ka watjanu "Muntauwa. Paluru wakantjaku kuraringkupai mununti palunyatjanungku Tjintulu nyuntunya wantinyi. Utin palumpa kalpariwa. Kulila! Kutjupa ara Tjintunya ngali malparara nyinangi, ka ngayulu mungawinki pakara kukaku ankuwiyangku wantinyangkampa paluru mapalku tjarpapai kana tjapa mapalku ngalkupai."

Ka watjanu Alitjilu, kulira, "Uwanti palu paltjatjiratja wiyangku awa?"

Ka Nyantjungku watjanu, "Uwa palu Tjintulu patalpai, ngayulu paltjatjiratjarintjaku."

Ka tjapinu Alitjilu, wayatjara pulka, ti: pulkatjara para-nyakula, "Wanyu nyuntu mulapa Tjintu markunu rawangku ti: tjikintjikitjangku?"

Ka watjanu Nyantjungku, "Wiya pungulinku mungatu, inmangka. Panya ngayulu inma inkangi:

Urungka tjarpara tjarpara
Urungka tjarpara tjarpara
Tjintu piratu patjapatjani.

"Ninti manti nyuntu inma palumpa."

Ka Alitjilu watjanu, "Inma kutjupa, palu purunypa ngayulu nganmantju kulinu." Ka Nyantjungku watjanu,

"Ka kampa kutjupa alatji:

Tjintjulu utulu utulu
Tjintjulu utulu utulu
Pintjantjaratu utulunanyi.

"No," said the Horse, "but the Sun waits there until we do get hungry."

Alitji looked at the large billy-can full of tea. "Have you really told the Sun to stay where it is, so that it will always be tea-time?"

The Stockman shook his head.

"No, we quarrelled some time ago over a song I was singing:

Once a jolly Stockman
Camped on a bull-ant nest
Under the shade of a kurrajong-tree.
And he sang as he brushed the
Bull-ants off his trouser-legs,
'I'd better douse these bugs here with tea.'
Camped on an ant-nest,
Camped on an . . .

Ka Kuwalangku anangu winki urira inkangu kunkunpa winkingku, "Urungka urungka urungka urungka . . ." rawa mulapa inkanyangka pula kata pungu wiyaringkuntjaku.

Ka piruku watjanu Nyantjungku, "Kana inma nguwanpa wiyaringkunyangka Kungkapa:ntu katu mirara watjanu, 'Tjintunya kuluntananyi paluru, kata katala'."

Ka watjanu Alitjilu, "Minyma pikati mantu."

Ka rawangku wangkangi Nyantjungku, "Katju palulanguru Tjintunya kuraringkupai mununi kutjupa ara tungunpungkupai munu rawa mulapa tjaru ngarapai."

Ka uwankara utiringu Alitjila, ka watjanu, "Muntauwa nyura wayatjara pulka ti: pulkatjara warungka tjunu tjintu tjarpara."

Ka Nyantjungku watjanu, "Uwala munula rawangku tjikilpai Tjintunya titutjara tjaru ngaranyangka."

Ka tjapinu, "Palu ti: wiyarampa awa?"

Ka Tjakumunungku tja:katira watjanu, "Ka:rkararinyina. Tjitjawa! Tjukurpa wangka!"

Ka kuntaringkula watjanu, "Wiya, ngurpa ngayulu."

Ka pula watjanu, "Ala Kuwala, nyuntu! Wankariwa!" Munu pula pungu.

Here the Koala shook itself and began to sing in its sleep: "Camped on a . . . camped on a camp . . ." and went on for so long that the other two had to hit it to make it stop.

"I'd almost finished my song," the Stockman went on, "when the Witch shouted 'He's murdering the Sun. Off with his head!' "

"What a savage woman!" Alitji exclaimed.

"So ever since then, the Sun won't do a thing I ask except on Sundays; he just stays in the one place all the time."

Alitji now understood it all and repeated, "I see, it's as I said—you've put this great quantity of tea on the fire because the Sun is always about to set."

"Yes," said the Horse, "and we just keep on drinking, because the Sun is always just about to set."

"But what happens when the tea is finished?" she asked.

The Stockman yawned and said, "I'm getting bored. Tell us a story, child!"

Rather alarmed, Alitji said, "I'm afraid I can't think of one."

So then they both cried, "Then *you* shall tell us a story, Koala. Wake up!" And they started to hit him, both together.

The Koala slowly opened its eyes and said in a feeble voice, "I wasn't asleep, I heard everything you were saying."

Ka kuru kutju purkarangku alara tjalymara watjanu, "Kunkunpa wiyangku ngayulu nyuranya kuliningi."
Ka watjanu Tjakumunungku, "Tjukurpa wangka."
Ka Nyantjungku watjanu, "Mapalku wangka—piruku kunkunarintjaku-tawara."
Ka Kuwalangku alatji wangkangu, "Ngura kutjupangka kunyu tjitji kungka mankurpa nyinangi, ini Tilinya, Iltjinya munu Itjilanya. Tjitji nyanga mankurpa tangkangka nyinangi . . ."
Ka Alitjilu tjapinu, "Nya:ya ngalkunu?"
Ka watjanu Kuwalangku, kulira kulira, "Mai tangka."
Ka urulyaranu munu piruku tjapinu, "Palu ya:ltjingara paunu?"
Ka watjanu, "Warungka mantu. Panya tili ngarangi."
Palu Alitjilu putu kulinu munu tjapinu piruku, "Palu tangkangkaya nya:ku nyinangi?"
Ka watjanu Tjakumunungku, "Ti: kutjupa tjikila."
Ka watjanu, "Ya:ltjingarana kutjupa tjikilku nganmantju tjikilwiya?"
Kaya pilunpa nyinangi, ka tjitjingku ti: mantjinu, mai kulu munu tjikira ngalkunu, munu piruku Kuwalangka tjapinu, "Palu tangkangkaya nya:ku nyinangi?"
Ka watjanu kulira kulira, "Tangka nyangatja ultukunpatjara."
Ka watjanu, "Iiiii wiya, nguntin wangkanyi."
Ka Nyantjungku pula pilunmanu, ka Kuwalangku mulyararira watjanu, "Ngunti wiya, mulamulangkuna wangkanyi. Ngayuku wantirampa nyuntu puta tjukurpa wangka."

"Tell us a story," said the Stockman.
"And be quick about it," added the Horse, "or you'll be asleep before you've started."
"In a far country" (the Koala began) "there were three little girls, all sisters, called Tili, Iltji and Itjila. All three lived in a tank."
"What did they live on?" Alitji asked.
"Cooked food," said the Koala.
Much surprised, Alitji said, "But how could they cook it?"
"On a fire, of course," said the Koala. "Don't forget they had Tili."
Alitji couldn't follow this and asked, "But why did they live in a tank?"
The Stockman said: "Have some more tea?"
"How can I have more," said Alitji, "when I've had nothing to begin with?"
No one answered, so she helped herself to some tea and damper, and then repeated her question. "Why did they live in a tank?"
The Koala took a while to think about it and then said: "It was a tank of nectar."
"It couldn't have been," began Alitji angrily; but the Horse and the Stockman hushed her, and the Koala said sulkily: "It was, and if you don't like my story you'd better tell your own."
"No, please go on," said Alitji humbly. "You are a wonderful story-teller and I won't interrupt again. Perhaps the tank was full of nectar after all."

The Koala's story was about three sisters — Tili, Iltji and Itjila — who lived in a tank.

Kuwala tjukurpa wangkangu. Kungka mankurpaya kunyu nyinangi tangkangka, ini Tilinya, Iltjinya, munu Itjilanya.

Ka kuntangku watjanu, "Munta. Ngurpa ngayulu, tjitji kura. Wanyu nyuntu wirungku piruku wangka, kana piluntu kulilku, wangkawiyangku. Mulapa manti tangka paluru ultukunpatjara."

Ka piruku Kuwalangku wangkangi, "Ka tangka iltjingka ngarangi."

Ka pakara watjanu Alitjilu, kalkuntja panyatja kulilwiyangku, "Wiya Iltjinya tangka unngu nyinangi."

Ka Kuwalangku watjanu—katungku, "Tangka nyangatja iltjingka ngarangi kaya kungka mankurtu tjatjara tjuta ngalkuningi."

Ka piruku watjanu Alitjilu, "Tangka unngu nyinaraya wanyu ngalkuningi?"

Ka watjanu "Uwa mantuya, tjanpi, tjanmata, tjata—tjatjara tjutaya ngalkuningi munuya tjala tjalantanangi, munu tjawu tjalatjunangi munuya tjalyngarangu."

Ka Alitjilu watjanu, "Palu nya:kuya tjatjara ngalkunu?"

Ka Kuwalanya tja:katira kuru pilupiluringu munu kunkunaringu, ka pula piruku pungu ka tjukutjuku mirara wankaringkula watjanu,"Tjatjara tjuta—tjalinpa tjaputjapu tjantjalku—wanyu nganalu nyura tjantjalku ngalkunu?"

Ka nyangatja uwankara putu alatjitu kulira watjanu, "Wampanti. Kulilwiya ngayulu."

Ka watjanu, "Ala, utin wankawiyatu nyinama."

Ka alatji kura wangkanyangka Alitjinya pakara ma-pitjangu pulkara tjanampa kuraringkula.

Ka Kuwala mapalku kunkunaringu, ka kutjupa kutjara watarku nyinangi munu malaku pitjantjaku altiwiya.

Ka Alitjilu ngalkikatira nyangu pulanya Kuwala wayatjarangka tjarpatjunkunyangka.

Mununku watjanu, "Palulakutu ngayulu malaku ankuwiyangku wantiku. Mulapaya kata kawakawa nyinanyi."

The Koala consented to go on. "And this tank was away out in the desert—"

Forgetting her promise, Alitji jumped up. "No, Iltji was in the tank!"

The Koala said very loudly: "The tank was in the desert and the three sisters had to eat everything that begins with a 't'."

"They ate all this while they were in the tank?" Alitji interrupted again.

"Yes," said the Koala, "tomtits, turkeys, tea-tree, anything that begins with a t. They chewed twigs and stewed thistles until they were satiated."

"Why did they eat things beginning with a 't'?" Alitji persisted.

The Koala yawned; its eyelids drooped; he fell asleep. But the other two hit it again, and with a little shriek it went on: "Everything that begins with a 't', turtles, tadpoles . . . wait, who's eaten a tadpole?"

Simply unable to understand any of this, Alitji said: "I don't think—"

"Then you shouldn't talk," said the Horse.

After this piece of rudeness, Alitji got up and walked away, quite unable to tolerate them any longer. The Koala immediately went to sleep and neither of the others took the least notice of her going, or called her back. The last time she looked behind her, they were dipping the Koala in the large billy-can.

"At any rate, I'll never go there again," Alitji said to herself. "They really are quite mad."

So saying, she noticed that one of the eucalyptus trees in front of her had a large hollow trunk, so she went closer, then crept inside, and found herself once more in the big cave with the little openings around the

Munu nyangatja watjara Alitjilu itara nyangu, itara tja:tjara, munu ma-ilaringkula tjarpangu munu tjarpara panya palunya nyangu, kulpi panya lipi, kalta katu ngarangi ala utju tjuta. Ka tjitjingku tji:lta tatira mai ngantja ngalkunu marangku rawangku kanyintjatjanungku. Munu tjukutjukuringkula ala utju wanu ma pakanu. ``Ngangari ngura nyangatja pika wiru alatjitu,'' munu para-ngarangi.

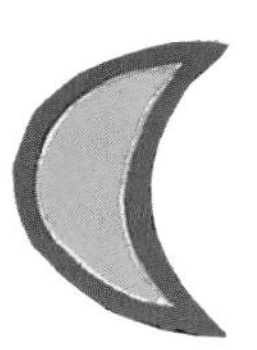

top. Alitji climbed on to the large root, ate some mistletoe berries, and when she was small enough, squeezed through the opening and at last found herself in that beautiful place she had been seeking for so long.

* For an explanation of the Pitjantjatjara names used in the Koala's story, please see the 'Notes on *Alitji*' at the back of this book.

Kungkapa:nku Kaimi

A*litjilu pakara* nyangu anangu Nyalpi mankurpa karungka nyinanyangka. Karkungkaya inuntji tjuta nyitiningi—warpungkulaya nyitiningi. Ka watjanu Nyalpi kutjungku, ``Wanti ngana. Ngayunyan ngunti nyitinu.''

``Munta. Nyangangkuni nyiku untunu.''

``Wiya ngayulu. Nya:kunin puntura watjani?''

Ka watjanu nganmanyitjangku, ``Pilunari. Tjaka nyuntu unytju pikaringkupai.''

Ka watjanu kutjupangku, ``Kulila! Nyuntu puta pilunari—Kungkapa:ntu nyuntunya kuluntanu.''

``Iiii—wiya. Nya:kuni?''

Ka watjanu, ``Nyuntu kunyu ainkura tjuta urara ungu palunya ngalkuntjaku. Ka mirpanaringu.''

Ka karku wanira pikaringkula watjanu, ``Kakari! Ainkura kuru wiru alatjitu ngayulu palumpa uranu. Kani nya:ku kuranmananyi?''

Munu paluru alatji wangkara Alitjinya nyangu, kaya uwankara palunya nyakula nyitilwiya pilunaringu. Ka kuntangku watjanu Alitjilu, ``Nya:ku nyura inuntji piranpa nyitini?''

Ka purkarangku watjanu, Nyalpi kutjungku, ``Kulila, kungka. Nganampa Mayatjangku tjuta altingu inma inkantjaku. Kaya kaimi inkaku tjirilya tjutangka. Palu Mayatja inuntji tjitintjitinku mukuringkupai, kala piranpa

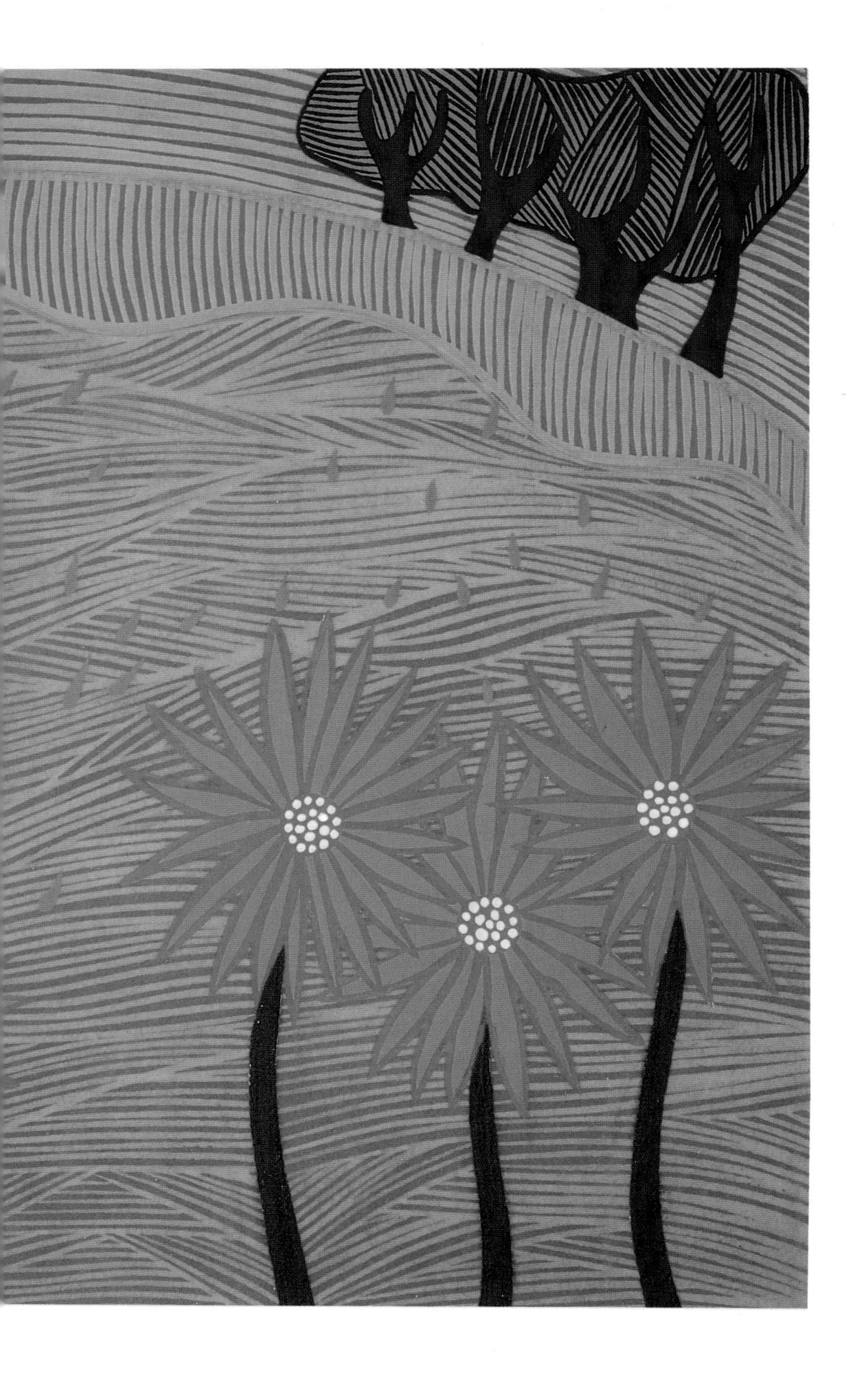

The Witch Spirit's Game

When she stood up and looked about her, Alitji saw three Leaf People in the creek-bed. They had a large supply of red ochre, which they were hastily splashing over a number of flowers and some unfortunate echidnas.. She heard one of the Leaf People say: "Look out, you, don't go splashing it all over me like that."

"Sorry," said the other, "this one bumped my elbow."

"That's right," complained the third Leaf Person, "always blame me."

"Quiet," said the first, "you get angry about nothing."

"I'd mind myself, if I were you," the second speaker said. "The Witch Spirit has said she'll have you beheaded."

"Rubbish!" the first Leaf Person retorted. "What for?"

"They say you gave her ainkura balls to eat, and of course they are poisonous, so she is very angry."

The first speaker threw down his ochre and complained angrily, "For crying out loud! Of all the unjust things! They were beautiful puff balls, ripe and powdery."

"Maybe," said the other, "but inedible." As he spoke, his glance fell upon Alitji. The other two followed his glance and, stopping what they were doing, fell silent.

Three Leaf People in the creek-bed were hastily splashing red ochre over flowers.

Anangu nyalpi mankurtu inuntji warpungkula nyitiningi.

nyanganpa nyitini mirpanarira ngananan ya kata katantjaku-tawara.''

Ka kutjupangku katu mirangu, ''Mayatja! Mayatja!''

Kaya anangu Nyalpi mankurpa punungka tatinu, munuya katu ngarangi, ka Alitjilu malakukutura nyangu anangu Nyalpi tjuta mulapa ngalya-ilaringkunyangka.

Tjitji tjutaya para-inkara kuranyu pitjangu, ka tjanala malangka nyinka tjuta, Kungkapa:nnga tjana. Ka ngururpa Malu Piranpa wangkarinangi Alitjinya nyakuwiya.

Ka Kungkapa:ntu Alitjinya nyakula ngarala watjanu, ''Ngananya nyangatja?'' Kaya pilunpa ngarangi. Ka watjanu, ''Tjitji, ini ngananyan?''

Ka kuntangku watjanu, ''Ngayulu Alitjinya.''

Ka wilitjunkula watjanu, ''Kaya ngananya tjana katu ngaranyi punungka?''

Ka watjanu Alitjilu, alipiri urira, ''Wampanti. Ngurpa ngayulu.''

Ka Kungkapa:nnga mirpanaringu pulkara munu mirara watjanu, ''Kata katala kata kata . . .''

Ka Alitjilu katu watjanu,''Wiya! Pilunari!'' Ka pilunaringu.

Ka Tjangaralu watjanu kuringka, ''Wanyu wanti. Ngaltutjara. Tjitji kutju nyangatja.''

Ka Alitjinya wantira Kungkapa:ntu panyanpa altingu, ''Ngalya-ukaliwaya.'' Kaya ukalingu, ka watjanu katu mulatu, ''Ngalya-ilariwa.'' Kaya purkara ilaringu. Ka Kungkapa:ntu inuntji tjuta karkutjara nyakula watjanu, ''Nya:ningi nyura tjananya?''

Ka purkara mulatu pupakatira watjanu, ''Nganana karkutja . . .''

''Would you tell me, please,'' Alitji began a little diffidently, ''why you are painting those flowers and echidnas?''

One of the Leaf People explained in a low voice: ''Listen, little girl, the Witch Spirit has invited a great crowd together. They are all going to play and dance using these echidnas as balls. Unfortunately, the Witch likes only red flowers, so we are painting these for fear that she will have us beheaded.''

Just then, one of the others shouted, ''The Witch Spirit! The Witch Spirit!''

The three Leaf People climbed hastily into a tree and hung there, and Alitji looked around, curious to see the Witch Spirit in person.

First came the Leaf Children, laughing and jumping about, followed by the young initiates, the Witch Spirit and others. The White Kangaroo was walking with a number of guests, talking hurriedly; he did not notice Alitji.

When the procession reached Alitji, however, they all stopped to stare at her. The Witch Spirit said in a severe tone of voice, ''Who is this?'' No one answered, so she said to Alitji, ''What is your name, child?''

''I am Alitji,'' Alitji replied very politely.

''And who are they?'' said the Witch, pointing to the Leaf People hanging in the tree.

''How should I know?'' said Alitji, shrugging her shoulders.

The Witch Spirit turned crimson with rage and started shouting: ''Off with her head, off with her head, off . . .''

The Leaf Children led the procession, followed by the young initiates, the Witch Spirit and others.

Tjitji tjutaya kuranyu pitjangu, ka tjanala malangka nyinka tjuta, Kungkapannga tjana.

Ka inuntji pulkara nyakula watjanu, "Kakari. Kata tjananya katala!"

Kaya uwankara ma-pitjangu, palu wati mankurpa Nyalpi ilunankuntjikita pitjangu, ka Alitjilu ngalturingkula langkaku pitingka tjananya kutitjunu kaya wati mankurtu putu ngurira kutjupa tjuta ma-wananu.

Ka Kungkapa:ntu mirangu, "Kata tjananyan katanu?"

Ka watjanu, "Kataya wiyaringu."

Ka palyanmanu, munu Alitjila tjapinu mirara, "Nyuntu kaimi inkapai tjaputjapungka?"

Ka watjanu, "Uwana."

Ka mirara watjanu, "Ala, ngalya-pitja!" Ka Alitjinya tjunguringkula tjanala ma-pitjangi.

Ka watjanu palula, wangka tjukutjukungku, "Ngura wiru nyangatja." Ka Alitjilu ngalkikatira Malu Piranpa nyangu, munu watjanu, "Uwa wiru mulapa. Ka Piriyitjanyampa?"

Ka Malu Pirantu iluruilurungku pupakatira pinangka ilaringkula tjalymara watjanu, "Palunya wangkawiyangku wantima. Kuluntanu palunya."

Ka watjanu Alitjilu, "Nyaku?"

"Kungkapa:nnga kata pungu." Ka Alitjinya katu mulapa ikaringu, ka Malungku para-nyakula watjanu ngulungulungku, "Pilunari. Kulila Piriyitjanya mala wirkanu ka Kungkapa:ntu watjanu . . ."

Ka katu mulatu Kungkapa:ntu watjanu, "Ala ririririwaya." Kaya unwankara yuruyuruningi munuyanku pungangi munuya ngula kutju ririringu.

Ka unwankara nyakula Alitjinya pulkara urulyaranu. Panya tjaputjapu wiyangkaya tjirilyangka inkangi, munuya tjananya pungangi tjulpu urutjangka. Kaya marangku tjinangku pana pampura pupangi wati tjuta, kaya tjanala wanu ma-pungangi tjirilya.

"Nonsense, be quiet!" Alitji said loudly; and the Witch Spirit fell silent.

The Cannibal said to the Witch Spirit quietly: "Consider, my dear, she is only a child."

The Witch turned angrily away, and called to the three Leaf People in the tree, "Come down!" So down they came. "Come over here!" she commanded. Reluctantly they moved closer. Then the Witch's eye fell on the echidnas, smothered in red ochre. "What have you been doing to them?" she demanded.

Hanging their heads, the Leaf People replied shamefacedly, "We were painting . . ."

The Witch had been looking hard at the echidnas. "So I see, so I see," she said, then: "Off with their heads!"

And, as the whole procession began to move away, three of the men remained behind to execute the unfortunate painters. But Alitji took pity on them and hid them in a rabbit hole, invisible in the rocks, until, unable to find them, the executioners went off after the others.

"Are their heads off?" shouted the Witch.

"Their heads are gone," the executioners replied.

"That's all right, then," the Witch said. Turning to Alitji, she shouted: "Do you know how to play games with balls?"

"Yes!" Alitji shouted back.

"Come on, then!" shouted the Witch, and so Alitji joined the procession.

"What a lovely place this is," a quiet voice beside her said, and, turning round, Alitji saw the White Kangaroo.

She answered: "Yes, it's beautiful. But tell me, where is the Spirit of the North Wind?"

Ka Alitjilu putu nguwantu kanyiningi tjulpu urutja, munu kunyu palunya palya witira, munu liri tjukarurura tjirilya putu nyangu, paluru ma-wirtjapakanyangka. Munu Alitjilu ngurira mantjira piruku panangka tjunkula putu pungu, urutja kata katuringkunyangka. Ka kunyu tjulpu paluru rawangku kata katuringkula Alitjinya mulya ilangku nyangangi ka Alitjinya putu alatjitu inkara ikaringangi pulkara.

Kaya kutjupa tjuta nguntingunti inkangi, munuyanku wangkara-waningi munuya tjirilya waltjatjara kutitjunangi, ka Kungkapannga pulkara mulapa mirpanarira para-kantuningi munu mirara watjaningi,

"Hush, hush," whispered the Kangaroo, looking anxiously over his shoulder. Then he whispered into her ear, "She is under sentence of execution."

"What for?" said Alitji.

"She hit the Witch over the head." Alitji gave a little scream of laughter. "Oh, hush," said the Kangaroo, looking around fearfully, "you see, she arrived late, and the Witch said—"

At that moment the Witch shouted: "Get ready, everyone!" And all the Leaf People and the host of small animals began to run about in all directions, bumping into each other and calling to one another, until at last they were all in position.

"Kata palunya katala", munu piruku watjaningi tjuta arangku, "Kata palunya katala." Ka Alitjinya nguluringu paluru wipiyarinyangka, munu urulyaranu wanka tjuta nyakula, panya tjuta mulapa paluru kuluntanangi.

Ka ankuntjikitjangku kulinu Alitjilu, munu para-nyangangi kampangkatu wirtjapakantjikitja, palu nyangu kutjupa, putu ngurkanankuntja ilkaringka ngaranyangka. Ka rawangku nyakuntjatjanungku ikaringkuntja nyangu, mununku kulinu, "Muntauwa, Ngaya piruku utiringanyi. Palya, kuwarilinku malpa nyinaku."

Ka tja:winki utiringkula watjanu, "Palyan nyangangka nyinanyi?"

Ka patanu pina utiringkuntjaku, kulira "Unytjungkuna wangkaku pina wiyangka. Putuni kulilku." Ka kuwaritu kata winki utiringu, ka Alitjilu tjulpu urutja walatjunu munu uwankara Ngayangka tjakultjunu, pukularira malpa pitjanyangka.

Munu watjanu, "Wangkarawanipai tjuta nyanganpa, kanatju putu kulini. Kaya tjirilya tjuta ankupai, watalpi pungkunyangka, kaya urutja tjuta kata uripai tjirilya pungkuwiyangku wantira, kaya winki alatjitu ngaltjurmankupai."

Ka tjalymara watjanu Ngayangku, "Ka Mayatjampa? Mukuringkupai palumpa nyuntu?"

Ka watjanu, "Wiya minyma nganyiriri alatjitu paluru, kana palumpa . . ."

Ka Alitjilu alatji watjanyangka Mayatja ilaringu ka Alitjilu pulkara nguluringkula watjanu, ". . . pulkara mukuringanyi."

Ka Kungkapa:nnga kanankananpa ikaringkula wati-pitjangu.

Alitji thought she had never seen such a strange sight. The balls for this game were the echidnas, and they were being hit with storks. The initiates had to double themselves up and stand on their hands and feet to make arches, through which the echidnas were hit. Alitji could scarcely hold her stork, and when she finally secured its body under her arm and straightened out its neck, her echidna had crawled away. She found it and brought it back and was about to give it a blow with the stork, but the tiresome bird kept twisting its head and looking into her face in a most provoking way. Alitji soon found that she couldn't play at all, and collapsed into helpless laughter.

The rest of the players were falling into a hopeless muddle, arguing and getting in one another's way, and taking one another's echidnas, while the Witch, becoming crosser and crosser, was stamping about, shouting: "Off with his head!" "Off with her head!" Alitji grew a little frightened, and was rather surprised to see so many people left alive.

She looked about, seeking some way of escape, and then she noticed a curious appearance in the air. After gazing at it for some time, she was able to make out a smile. "It's the Wild Cat!" she thought. "That's good, now I'll have a friend."

When the whole mouth had appeared, the Wild Cat said: "How are you getting on?"

Alitji waited for his ears to appear, thinking, "It's no use speaking until the ears have appeared, for he'll never hear me." Then, releasing her stork, she began to explain things to him.

The balls for this game were echidnas and they were being hit with storks.

Panya tjaputjapu wiyangkaya tjirilyangka inkangi munuya tjananya pungangi tjulpu urutjangka.

Ka Tjangarula pitjala tjapinu, "Nyuntu nganala wangkanyi, awa?"

Ka watjanu, "Ngayuku malpangka, Ngaya palangka."

Ka Tjangaralu watjanu, "Ngangka, mamu alatjitu."

Ka Ngayangku watjanu, "Unan!"

Ka Tjangaralu Alitjila kumpinu munu watjanu, "Kuran wangkangu. Awa nya:kunin alatji nyanganyi kuru pulkangku?" Munu Kungkapa:nnga altira watjanu, "Kuri putitja, Ngaya nyanga wiyala."

Ka nyakuwiyangku watjanu, "Kata katala."

Ka Tjangaralu watjanu, "Kata katalpaina altiku," munu mapalku anu.

Ka Alitjinya malaku anu kaimiku, palu Kungkapa:nnga kutju kulinu, pikati alatjitu mirawaninyanyangka, kaya tjuta kinkinmara yuruyuruningi wati tjuta ka kaimi winki kuraringu, ka Alitjilu ma-pitjala palumpa tjirilya ngurinu

"Everyone here argues so. I can't hear myself speak, and the echidnas crawl away before one can hit them, and the storks refuse to keep their heads down, and everyone just complains and complains."

"How do you like the Witch?" asked the Wild Cat in a low voice.

"Not at all," Alitji answered. "She's such a savage woman, and I—"

As she said this, the Witch Spirit herself drew near, so Alitji finished lamely, "—like her very much."

The Witch passed on, smiling proudly.

"Who are you talking to?" asked the Cannibal Spirit, coming up to Alitji.

"To my friend, the Wild Cat," Alitji told him.

"Good heavens, an evil spirit!" said the Cannibal. "But it may kiss my hand if it likes."

"I'd rather not," the Wild Cat remarked.

At this, the Cannibal Spirit hid behind Alitji and said, "Don't be impertinent and don't look at me like that, with those big eyes." Then he called to the Witch and said: "My dear, I wish you would have this Wild Cat removed."

Without looking round, the Witch shouted: "Off with his head!"

"I'll fetch the executioner," said the Cannibal Spirit, and hurried off.

Alitji thought she might as well go back to see how the game was progressing. She could hear the Witch's voice in the distance, screaming with rage, and as she got closer everyone else seemed to be running about in confusion, giving orders and arguing, so that the whole game was pandemonium. Alitji went off to find her echidna, but it was fighting with another echidna, and palu tjirilya kutjupanku pula pika pungangi, ka piruku ankula urutja palumpa nyangu apu katu nyinanyangka. Munu tatira mantjira malakungku katingu palu tjirilya panya kutjara putu nyakula Ngaya kutu ma-pitjangu.

Munu para pitjala nyangu anangu nyalpi mungilyi alatjitu tjunguringkula ira-nyakunyangka. Uwankaraya wangkawiya ngarangi palu wati kata katalpaingku pulkara wangkangi Kungkapa:nta Tjangarala pulala.

Watingku alatji wangkangi, "Puntu wiyangka ngayulu ya:ltjingara kata katalku?"

Tjangaralu alatji wangkangi, "Kata pala ngaranyi kan puta katani." Kungkapa:ntu alatji wangkangi, "Mapalkuya nya:la. Kuwarina anangu uwankara kuluntananyi."

Kaya Nyalpi uwankara iluruilururingu.

Ka watjanu Alitjilu, "Piriyitjaku Ngaya palatja. Palunyaya puta alti."

Ka Kungkapa:ntu watjanu, "Ma-alti!" Ka wati kata katalpai ma-tarararingu.

Ankunyangka Ngaya kata arkayiringu, ka Tjangaralu para-wirtjapakara nguriningi kaya kutjupa tjuta kaimiku malaku anu.

her stork was standing on top of a rock. Climbing up, she retrieved it, but by the time she got back with it, the echidna had disappeared, so she released it again and went back to the Wild Cat.

She was surprised to find quite a crowd of Leaf People staring up at it, all silent. The executioner was disputing with the Spirit Parents.

"I can't cut off a head if there's no body to cut it off from," the Executioner was saying.

And the Cannibal Spirit was saying, "There's the head—so cut it off!"

The Witch was shouting, "Everybody do something, or I'll have you all beheaded!"

All the Leaf People shuffled anxiously.

Alitji said, "The Wild Cat belongs to the Spirit of the North Wind. You'd better ask her about it."

"Call her," ordered the Witch, and the executioner hurried off.

The moment he had gone, the Wild Cat's head began fading away. The Cannibal Spirit ran wildly up and down, looking for it, while everyone else went back to the game.

Malumaluku Tjukurpa

K*a watjanu Piriyitjalu*, ''Ngangari, pukularinyina piruku nyuntunya nyakula,'' munu ngalikitikitira palula mapitangi.

Ka Alitjinya kulu pukularingu paluru pukularinyangka. Mununku kulinu, ''Muntauwa itunytju mantu palunya kuranu, ka kuwari mirpanpa wiyaringu. Tjinguru iruwa kuwari tjikintjatjanu paluru tjuwitariku.''

Ka watjanu Piriyitjalu, ''Pulkara kulintjatjanungku nyuntu wangkawiyangku wantinyi.''

Ka watjanu mapalku, ''Munta, kaimi wiruya inkanyi.''

Ka Piriyitjalu ngutu tjunu Alitjila alipiringka munu wakaningi palunya ngutu iringku, palu payiliyangku wantingu Alitjilu.

Ka piruku painu Piriyitjalu, ''Piruku nyuntunku kulini munun wangkawiyangku wantinyi.''

Ka Alitjilu watjanu, palumpa kuraringkula, ''Palya mantu ngayulu kulinma.''

Ka watjanu, ''Uwa, kaya palya mantu kanyala parpakanma, kaya punu tjuta para-pitjama, kaya . . .''

Palu wangka paluru wiyaringu, ka Alitjinya urulyarara ira-nyangu, munu nyangu Kungkapannga anga-ngarala walu-nyakunyangka.

Ka wangka upangku Piriyitjalu watjanu, tjitingkula, ''Tjintu wiru awa.''

The Kangarurtle's Story

''Y*ou can't imagine* how glad I am to see you again,'' the North Wind Spirit said as she tucked her arm into Alitji's and they walked off together.

Alitji was very glad to find her in such a pleasant temper, and thought to herself that perhaps it was only the intunypa root that had made her so hot-tempered. ''Perhaps,'' Alitji thought, ''if she were to drink some honey water she would become really sweet-tempered.''

Suddenly the Spirit of the North Wind said, ''You are thinking so much that you have forgotten to speak.''

''I'm sorry,'' Alitji said quickly. ''It's a very interesting game they are playing, isn't it?''

The Spirit of the North Wind rested her chin on Alitji's shoulder. It was an uncomfortably sharp chin, but not wanting to be rude, Alitji said nothing.

Now the North Wind Spirit chided Alitji again. ''You are still thinking and saying nothing.''

''I have a right to think,'' Alitji said sharply.

''Just as much right as Blue-tongued Lizards have to fly, or trees to wander—''

To Alitji's surprise, the voice of the North Wind Spirit trailed off at this point; looking up, she saw the Witch Spirit barring the way, glaring down on them both.

The North Wind Spirit and Alitji walked off arm in arm.
Piriyitjanya pula Alitjinya mapitjangu.

Ka pulkara kantura katu alatjitu mirangu, ''Ma-pitja! Kuwarinanta kata katani.''
Ka mapalku ma-wiyaringu.
Ka Kungkapa:ntu Alitjinya witunu, ''Ala, malaku pitja kala kaimi piruku inkama.'' Ka ngulungku ma-wananu Alitjilu.
Palu Nyalpi uwankaraya paku wiyaringangi wiltjangka, munuya Mayatja pitjanyangka nyakula pakara piruku inkangu.
Ka Kungkapa:nnga putu wantira rawa mirara waningi munu kuluntanangi munu kutjupa tjutangka wangkara wanira painingi, kaya anangu Nyalpi mankuraringu, panya tjutaya ma-katingu iluntankuntjikitjangku.
Ka Kungkapa:ntu watjanu, ''Nyuntu Malumalu nyangu?''
Ka tjitjingku watjanu, ''Wiyana.''
Ka watjanu minymangku, ''Ngalya-pitja, ka tjukurpa palumpa watjalku.''
Ka pula anu, ka Tjangaralu tjalymara watjanu anangu Nyalpingka, ''Uwankara walatjura. Kalypariwala.'' Ka Alitjinya kulira pukularingu.
Ka pula ma-pitjala nyangu tjintungka kunkunarinyangka. Kalaya. Ka Kungkapa:ntu nyutura katu watjanu, ''Wankariwa! Tjitji nyanga Malumalu nyakuntjaku kati, tjukurpa palumpa kulintjakutu.'' Munu wangkara ma-pitjangu.
Ka Kalayangku pakara watjanu, Alitjila, ''Wala!''
Ka kulinu, Alitjilu, ''Tjakangkuya witulpai, ngura nyangangka,'' munu ma-wananu.
Ka pula tjukutjuku ankula nyangu apu murpungka nyinanyangka Malumalu. Lutju alatjitu paluru

Trembling a little and in a weak voice, the Spirit of the North Wind said: ''It's a lovely day.''
''Be off, or your head will be!'' roared the Witch, stamping her foot.
The North Wind Spirit was off in a moment.
''Come, get on with the game,'' said the Witch to Alitji; and in fear and trembling, she followed the Witch Spirit back to the game.
The Leaf People were resting in the shade, but the moment they saw the Witch they hurried back to the game.
All the time they were playing, the Witch never stopped shouting and quarrelling, and ordering people's heads off, so that in no time there was scarcely anyone left in the game.
Then the Witch Spirit said to Alitji: ''Have you seen the Kangarurtle yet?''
''No,'' answered Alitji.
''Come on, then,'' said the Witch. ''He will tell you his story.''
As the two of them left, Alitji heard the Cannibal Spirit whisper to a Leaf Man, ''Let them all go, they are pardoned.'' She felt quite relieved.
Soon they came upon an Emu, asleep in the sun. The Witch Spirit prodded him and said loudly, ''Wake up! Take this child to see the Kangarurtle and hear his story.'' And then she walked away.
The Emu got up and said: ''Come on!''
''Everybody says 'Come on' here,'' thought Alitji.
She followed the Emu, and they had not gone far before they saw the Kangarurtle in the distance, sitting

Alitji and the Witch Spirit found the Emu asleep in the sun.

Kalaya kunkunpa ngaringi tjintungka, ka pula nyangu palunya, Alitjilu, Kungkapantu.

tjiturutjituru nyinangi, ka pula yainyangka kulinu ilaringkula, munu kuru ilantjara nyangu. Ka Alitjilu ngalturingkula watjanu, "Nya:ringu awa, tjiturutjiturarintjaku?"

Ka watjanu Kalayangku, "Wiya. Unytju paluru ulapai. Wala!"

Ka pula wirkanu ka Kalayangku palula watjanu, "Kungka nyangatja nyuntumpa tjukurpa kulintjikitja mukuringanyi."

Ka Malumalungku watjanu ula winkingku, "Ala watjalkuna. Nyinakati pula, munu wangkawiyangku kulinma."

Ka pula nyinakatingu ka pilunpa nyinangi ka ka:rka:raringu Alitjinya, patara patara.

Ka ngula kutju wangkangu, rawa ulantjatjanu. Alatji wangkangu: "Kuwaripatjara mulapa ngayulu malu mulapa nyinangi."

Alatjitu wangkangu, kaya piruku pilunpa nyinangi, palu ulangi kutju Malumalu, ka Kalaya kaltarapungu.

Ka ngula watjanu, "Kalanya kulunykulunypa tjuta Kanyalangku kanyiningi. Kala palunya ininu Kanyilanya."

Ka watjanu Alitjilu, "Nya:ku nyura Kanyilanya wangkangu? Kanyala alatjitu paluru."

Ka watjanu, "Ngananya kanyinyangka mantu. Ngurpa nyuntu."

sad and lonely on the top of a hill. As they came nearer, Alitji could hear his wailing and see that his eyes were filled with tears. She pitied him deeply and said to the Emu, "What is his sorrow?"

The Emu said: "He has no sorrow. It is all his fancy. Come on."

They approached the Kangarurtle and the Emu said to him, "This young lady wishes to hear your story."

"I shall tell it to her," said the Kangarurtle, his voice extremely tearful. "Sit down, both of you, and don't speak a word until I've finished."

They sat down and for some time nobody spoke, so that Alitji became bored, just waiting and waiting.

At last the Kangarurtle said, after a deep sigh, "In the beginning, I was a real Kangaroo."

These words were followed by a long silence, broken only by the sobbing of the Kangarurtle and an occasional belch from the Emu.

"When we were little," the Kangarurtle eventually went on, "our teacher was an old Turtle—we used to call him Tortoise."

"Why did you call him Tortoise, if he wasn't one?" Alitji asked.

"We called him Tortoise because he taught us," said the Kangarurtle angrily. "Really, you are very dull!"

Ka pula pulkara nyangangi Alitjinya ka kuntaringu, ngaltutjara. Ka Kalayangku watjanu Malumalungka, ''Ala wangkama, ngana. Malaringanyi nyanga.''

Ka watjanu, ''Kala uru lipingka itingka nyinangi, munula paki piranta inma tjuta inkangi. Panya Kanyilalu nintinu kala tjuta inkangi.''

Ka Alitjilu tjapinu, ''Wanyuni inma tjakultjura.''

Ka watjanu, ''Tjutala ngarala wanara kantunu, pititjalili, walputi, antipina, tutulpa, kutjupa tjuta kulu kaya tjarangku tjapurpungu, kaya tjara lakanu.''

Ka Kalayangku pakara pukularira watjanu, ''Uwala, munula kaputurira ma-kantura wararakatingu.''

Ka Malumalungku watjanu, ''Munula antipina wipu witira ma-rungkanu kaya urungka punkara ma-wiyaringu.''

Ka Kalayangku watjanu, pulkara pukularira, ''Ngangari, inma wiru, munula uwankara urungka tjarpara antipina ma-wananu, uru ngati pulkakutu.''

Ka Malumalungku katu mirara watjanu, ''Malaku aruriwa! Kala malaku pitjangu pana piltikutu.'' Munu pilunaringu, munu purkarangku wangkangu, ''Ka alatjitu wiyaringu.'' Munu ulangu piruku.

They both looked scornfully at Alitji, who felt most uncomfortable. At last the Emu said, ''Well go on, old fellow. It's getting late.''

''We lived beside the great water, and we used to dance on the white sand. It was the Turtle who taught us to dance.''

''What sort of dancing?'' Alitji asked.

''Why,'' said the Kangarurtle, ''you form a line along the shore—scorpions, fishes, turtles, everybody—and some beat time and others clap sticks.''

''That's right!'' cried the Emu enthusiastically, ''and then you all move into the centre together and stamp your feet and jump back.''

''And then, you know,'' went on the Kangarurtle, ''you take the fishes by their tails—''

''And hurl them out to sea!'' the Emu interrupted excitedly. ''Oh, it's a wonderful dance, really wonderful. Then we all swim after them, as far out as we can.''

''And back to land again,'' cried the Kangarurtle. ''And then it's finished,'' he added, suddenly dropping his voice.

At this, both he and Emu, who had been capering about all this time, sat down again very sadly and quietly, and looked at Alitji.

Ka Alitjilu watjanu, ''Ngangari inma wiru.''
Ka Malumalungku watjanu, ''Nyuntu nyakuntjikitja mukuringanyi?''
Ka watjanu, ''Uwana.''
Ka pulanku mara witira para-nyanpingu, munu Alitjinya tjina tjuta arangku kantuningi munu pula kantura purkarangku tjiturutjitururungkutu inma nyangatja inkangu:

Pititjalilila kulira wananu:
Pala palulala tjanangka tatinu.

Pala palulala tjanangka tatingi;
Yirkilayirkilalala ngarangi.

Paki wantira mantila
Uru pulkangka nyanpinyanpini.

Nyarkulpungkula nganana
Panya palula kuranyu
Malumalu inkanyi.

Pititjaliratjalira ngarala
Pititjalilingka inkanyi.

Kalaya urungka wanirala
Wanmayularuyularu.

Tjutiranguya ngarala
Uru katungka kurungkaringu.

''It must indeed be a lovely dance,'' she ventured timidly.
''Would you like to see it?'' asked the Kangarurtle.
''Very much indeed,'' said Alitji.
So, taking hands, they began solemnly to dance around Alitji, every now and then treading on her toes, and as they danced they sang this song, slowly and sadly:

We heard the little scorpions a-scurry on the sand,
And we climbed at once on to their scaly backs;
We left the beach behind us as we gamed towards the blue;
(Will you swim a little faster, get a hurry on, do!).

You can really have no notion how delightful it can be
To ride a deadly scorpion out to sea.
But the Kangarurtles stood upon the shore and cooled their heads
By showering them with sand, as custom says.

The numbats raised their tails above their soft and stripey fur,
And called the swimmers back to join the game;
But they threw the emus out to join the others in the deep,
And the Spirit of the North Wind looked askance.

She changed the numbats into rainbows and they glowed above the waves
Before she hurled them out on to the plain;
The fish with feathered head-dresses peered up from in their caves,
But promptly disappeared in fear again.

Piriyalutja rungkara wanani,
Kurpa maringkaliya anama.

Pintjukatiraya antipina kumpinu.
Ngunti mantuya kakalyalya murutjunu.

Malakukutu tjutukatingu:
Tutul panya palunyaya
Kulpara nyawa.

'Tutul wanyulanya mantjira kati;
Kurunywiyaringkulala karulu katinyi'.

Ka Alitjinya pukularingu, inma wiyaringkunyangka, munu watjanu, ''Ngangari, inma wirura inkangu, munu wirutu nyanpingu.''

Ka watjanu Kalayangku, ''Nya: palatja kinkinmananyi? Kulila.''

Ka ngarala kulinu.

Ka watjanu Kalayangku, ''Punturaya watjani. Wala!'' Munu Alitjinya mara witira ma-wirtjapakanu, Malumalu wantira, munu pula pararirira palunya ulanyangka kutju kulinu.

'Oh turtles, come and find us, come and take us to the shore,
We are drowning as our spirits fly away.
See how eagerly the snails and the numbats all advance—
They are coming from the plain to join the game'.

''It's a perfectly lovely song, and you dance very beautifully,'' Alitji said, relieved that it was over.

''What's that uproar? Listen!'' said the Emu.

And they listened.

''They're accusing him!'' the Emu said. ''Come on!'' And, taking Alitji's hand, be began to run, leaving the Kangarurtle behind. As they got farther away, they could hear his melancholy wailing ever more faintly.

Alitjinya Wankaringkuntja

Wirkara nyangu Alitjilu pula, Kungkapannga Tjangaranya warungka nyinanyangka. Kaya kutjupa tjuta kulukulu itilkira itilkira nyinangi, kuka kutjupa kutjupa tjuta, kaya tjulpu tjuta katu nyinangi punungka: kilykilykari, kurparu, itatura, wilyurukuruku, parkapungku, mungilyiya punu parkangka nyinara walu-nyangangi. Ka patu nyinangi, punu watangka, wati panya inuntji nyitilpai, ka kutjarangku, kulatatjarangku palunya karpira kanyiningi. Malu Piranpa Tjangarala itingka nyinangi, kaya anangu uwankara tjungu wangkangi katu mulapa munuya kinkinmanangi.

Ka pakara pilunmanu Malu Pirantu, kaya pilunaringu.

Ka Tjangaralu watjanu, "Nya:nu paluru?"

Ka Malungku katu watjanu, tjutangka mirangka ngarala, "Tjakumunuku Nyantju paluru kutitjunu."

Ka Mayatjangku watjanu, "Kata katala."

Ka Malu Pirantu watjanu, "Wiya, kuwaripa. Utila tjuta kulinma wararangku, kantiya tjarangku ngalkilariku." Munu altira watjanu, "Pitjalaya puntura wangka."

Ka pitjangu Nyantjutjara wati panya Tjakumunu. Kuwala kulu katu nyinangi, kunkunpa, munu paluru ukalingu wankaringkula munu Alitjila itingka nyinakatingu, warungka. Ka Tjakumunungku mai kanyiningi, wayatjara kulu, munu wirkara Nyantjungka nyinara nyangangi anangu tjuta, palu Kungkapa:nnga

Alitji Awakes

The Witch and the Cannibal were seated by the fire when Alitji and the Emu arrived at the place where all the commotion was happening. A great crowd had assembled about them, all sorts of creatures, large and small. And above, in the branches of the trees, perched hundreds of birds of every kind: budgerigars, magpies, hawks, parrots, cockatoos, all looking down. Sitting apart, at the foot of a big gum tree, was one of the Leaf men who had been painting the echidnas. Two others guarded him with spears. The White Kangaroo, looking very important, stood near the Cannibal Spirit, and everyone was talking loudly and excitedly.

Then the White Kangaroo stood up in front of them all and called for silence.

"What has the prisoner done?" said the Cannibal Spirit.

"He stole the Stockman's Horse," said the White Kangaroo.

"Off with his head!" shrieked the Witch.

"Not yet," the White Kangaroo suggested hastily. "Let us hear the evidence; indeed, some may speak on his behalf. Come forward, if anyone has an accusation to make," he called.

The mad Stockman appeared, riding the Horse, with the Koala seated in front of him—asleep, of course. The

A great crowd had assembled.

Tjuta mulapaya pitjangu.

nyakula nguluringu.

Ka Tjangaralu watjanu, ''Walangku wangka. Kuwarinanta kunakuluni, nguluringkunyangka.''

Ka nyanga palunyatjanu pulkara mulapa milypararanu munu putu wangkara mai wiya wayatjara ngunti patjanu, ka ngakanu, ka pulkara kuntjulpungu.

Ka Alitjinya kutjuparingu, mununku watjanu, ''Nya:ringuna? Muntauwa, pirukuna pulkaringanyi.''

Ka palula itingka Kuwala nyinangi, munu watjanu, ''Ma-paturiwa, utjuninin, putu nguwanpana nga:kampanyi.''

Ka kuntangku watjanu, ''Munta, watarkungkunanta utjunu, pulkaringkuntjatjanungku.''

Ka paira watjanu, ''Ngura nyangangkan uti pulkaringkuwiyangku wantima.''

Ka Alitjilu watjanu, ''Nya:kunin kuranmananyi? Nyuntu kulu pulkaringanyi.''

Ka Kuwalangku watjanu, ''Uwa mantu palu purkara mulapa ngayulu. Nyuntu mapalku kurkara purunyaringu.'' Munu mulyara pakara wararakatira warungka munkara nyinakatingu milpalingka.

Ka Tjangaralu watjanu, ''Ngangka:! Nya:ku nyuntu rawa alatjitu wangkawiya nyinanyi? Wangka! Mapalku wangka, kunakuluntjaku-tawara.''

Ka ulkarurira watjanu Tjakumunungku, ''Awarinatju, ngayulu ngurpa. Ngaltutjara ngayulu, awari ngalturiwatju. Kulila mungatula ti: tjikiningi ka Nyantjungku watjanu . . .''

Ka katu watjanu Nyantjungku, ''Wiya ngayulu! Nguntin wangkanyi.''

Stockman held some damper in one hand and a billy-can in the other, and sat there looking at the crowd. When his glance fell on the Witch Spirit, he became fearful. The Koala suddenly woke up, sleepily climbed off the Horse, and went to sit beside Alitji.

"Speak up," said the Cannibal Spirit. "I shall have you executed if you are nervous."

This only made the Stockman feel worse; his stomach contracted with fear. In his confusion, he bit a large piece out of the billy-can instead of the damper, and it stuck in his throat. He began to cough.

At that moment, Alitji felt a very curious sensation, which puzzled her at first. And then she realized what it was—"Of course! I'm starting to grow again!"

"I wish you wouldn't squeeze so," said the Koala. "I can hardly breathe."

"I can't help it," Alitji replied very meekly, "I'm growing, you see."

"You have no right to grow *here*," said the Koala.

"What nonsense," said Alitji, more boldly. "You are growing too, you know."

"Yes, but I grow at a reasonable pace," said the Koala, "not in that ridiculous fashion. You are already as tall as a desert oak." And he got up very sulkily and went over to the other side of the fire, where he sat next to a goanna.

"Are you going to sit there for ever?" the Cannibal Spirit asked the Stockman. "Speak up, or I'll have you executed at once."

Left: *The Koala was riding on the Horse, asleep as usual.*
Right: *In his confusion, the Stockman bit a large piece out of the billy-can.*

Tjampu: *Kuwala Nyantjungka tatira kunkunaringu — panya tjaka paluru kunkunaripai.* Waku: *Ka Tjakumunu milpararanu munu wayatjara ngunti patjanu mai palku.*

Ka Tjakumunungku watjanu, "Mulapa, nyuntu wangkangu alatjitu!"

Ka Nyantjungku piruku watjanu, "Wiya ngayulu."

Ka Tjangaralu watjanu, "Wiyanmanu paluru."

Ka piruku watjanu Tjakumunungku, "Kuwalangku watjanu." Munu palunya iluruilurungku nyangu, palu wiyanmankuwiyangku wantingu, kunkunarira.

Ka rawangku wangkangi Tjakumunungku, "Ka palula malangka ngayulu mai kutjupa ngalkunu."

Ka Warutjulyaltu watjanu, "Palu Kuwalangku nya: watjanu?"

Ka Tjakumunungku watjanu, "Wampa. Watarkuringu, ngayulu."

Ka Tjangaralu watjanu, "Watarkuriwiyangku kulinma. Kuwarinanta kukanmananyi."

Ka Tjakumunungku mai, pingkila kulu punkatjingara tjititingkula watjanu, "Awarinatju, ngurpa ngayulu. Ngalturiwatju, awari."

Ka wayutangku lakanu ka kukakarangku tja: katingu, kaya tjara milpatjunangi, kaya tjara pakara ma-ngarala wipu untjunaringu.

Ka Tjangaralu watjanu Tjakumunungka, "Ala wiyaringkulampa puta ma-pitja." Ka pakara punu kurkungka mapalku ma-wiyaringu.

Ka Kungkapantu watjanu, "Ka kata wiyala," palu putuya ma-nyangangi.

Ka Tjangaralu watjanu, "Kutjupa alti puntura wangkantjaku."

Ka minyma panyatja mai paulpai ngalya-pakanu.

Ka wangkantjaku witunu Tjangaralu, palu watjanu mulyarangku, "Wantinyina."

"I'm a poor man," the Stockman began in a trembling voice. "I know nothing about all this. Have pity on me. I was just drinking tea the other day with the Horse when he said—"

"I didn't, he's lying," the Horse interrupted loudly.

"You did," said the Stockman.

"I didn't," said the Horse.

"He denies it," said the Cannibal Spirit.

"Well, the Koala said—" went on the Stockman, looking anxiously at the Koala; but he denied nothing, for he was fast asleep.

"After that," the Stockman continued, "I ate some more damper."

"But what did the Koala say?" demanded the Goshawk.

"I can't remember," said the Stockman.

"You must remember," the Cannibal Spirit told him, "or I shall have you executed."

The miserable Stockman dropped his damper and his billy-can and said, shaking with fear, "I know nothing. I'm a poor man. Oh, dear!"

The crowd became restless. The Possum began to clap sticks, the Black Cormorant yawned. Some of them began to clear a space for story-telling, while others stood up and warmed their tails by the fire.

"If you have nothing more to say, you may go," said the Cannibal Spirit at last, and the Stockman galloped off into the mulga without waiting another second.

"And take off his head!" shouted the Witch Spirit; but the Stockman was already out of sight.

"Call somebody else!" said the Cannibal Spirit.

The Stockman galloped off into the mulga without waiting another second.

Ka Tjakumunu mapakara punu kurkungka mapalku mawiyaringu.

Ka Malu Pirantu watjanu Tjangarala, "Wanyu puta tjapinma palula."
Ka tjapinu alatji, Tjangaralu, "Mai nya: nyuntu pauningi?"
Ka watjanu, "Itunypa."
Ka Kuwalangku watjanu, "Ultukunpa."

Ka Kungkapantu mirangu, "Kuwala palaja witila. Kuwala palatja kata katala. Paila palatja, mulya katara wiyala."
Kaya winki alatjitu pakara yuruyuruningi, munuyanku wangkangi, munuya kuwala witira ma-katira punungka tjunu, munuya malaku pitjala minyma panya mai paulpai putu nyangu.
Ka Tjangaralu watjanu, "Kutjupa alti puntura wangkantjaku."
Ka pakara altingu Malungku, "Alitji."
Ka pakara ngarala, katu watjanu, Alitjilu, "Nyangangkana!" Palu Alitjinya pulkaringu, munu pakara nguwanpa pu:ntanu tjukutjuku tjuta; ka itjaritjari warungka nguwanpa punkanu; ka Alitjilu tjinangku watarkungku nganngi kantunu, ka ngaurmanu.

The next witness was the woman who had been so busy cooking in the North Wind Spirit's wurlie.
"Give your evidence," said the Cannibal Spirit.
"Shan't," said the woman.
"You'd better ask her some questions," the White Kangaroo suggested.
"What do you cook?" asked the Cannibal Spirit.
"Itunypa roots mostly," said the woman.
"Honey," muttered the Koala, stirring in his sleep.

"Collar that Koala," the Witch shrieked. "Cut off his head! Cut off his nose! Throw him out!"
At this, the whole crowd was thrown into confusion, jumping up, running around, calling out, and taking hold of the Koala and putting him in a tree. By the time they had settled down again, the woman who had been giving evidence was nowhere to be seen.
"Call the next witness," the Cannibal Spirit ordered.
Rising to his feet, the White Kangaroo called: "Alitji!"
"Here!" cried Alitji, jumping up. But she had grown so very large, and she jumped up in such a hurry, that she knocked over many small creatures, so that some were squashed, a desert mole was almost pushed into the fire, and a frog croaked as she trod on it.

Ka pulkara kuntaringkula Alitjilu watjanu, "Awari, munta, ngaltutjara." Munu warpungkula mantimantjiningi munu tjananya nyinatjunangi.

Ka uwankara piruku palyaringkunyangka Tjangaralu watjanu Alitjila, "Ala, nyuntu nya: kulinu nyanga palunya?"

Ka watjanu, "Wiya. Ngayulu ngurpa alatjitu."

Ka watjanu Tjangaralu, "Wara uwankara, kililpi kutu ngarantja, ma-pakala."

Alitjinya nyakula watjanu, kaya uwankarangku Alitjinya nyangangi.

Ka watjanu, "Ngayuluna wara, kililpi kutu, wiya."

Ka Tjangaralu watjanu, "Mulapa nyuntu."

Ka Kungkapantu watjanu, "Anangu Nyalpi pala kutitjunkupai ngalya-kati!"

Ka pula ngalya-katingu. Ka Kungkapantu watjanu, "Kata katala!"

Ka Alitjilu watjanu, "Wiya! Wanti! Nya:ku nyura puntura watjani palunya?"

Ka Malu Pirantu watjanu, "Nyantju mantu kutitjunu paluru."

Ka Alitjilu wilitjura watjanu, "Nyaratja mantu Nyantju kuwari ma-pitjangu Tjakumunu pula, ngananala uwankarangka mirangka."

Ka Kungkapantu mirara watjanu, "Pilunari!"

"Oh, I beg your pardon," she exclaimed in a tone of great dismay. "You poor little things!" And she began to pick them up and set them to rights as quickly as she could.

As soon as they had all recovered from the shock of being upset, the Cannibal Spirit said to Alitji: "What have you heard about this matter?"

"Nothing," she answered. "I know nothing at all about it."

Suddenly the Cannibal said, "Everyone very tall, who reaches up to the stars, must leave at once."

He looked at Alitji as he spoke, and everyone else turned to look at her too.

"I am not as high as the stars," Alitji said.

"You are," said the Cannibal Spirit.

"Bring the thief to me!" shouted the Witch.

They brought him from under the gum tree.

"Cut off his head!" she shrieked.

"Stop!" cried Alitji, "this is nonsense. What has he done?"

"He stole the Stockman's Horse," said the Kangaroo.

"Rubbish!" said Alitji. "The Stockman has just ridden off on his Horse in front of everyone here."

Ka katu watjanu, "Wantinyina!"

Ka mulya tjitintjitinarira mirara watjanu, Kungkapantu, "Kata katala!"

Kaya uwankara winki tiwilaringu.

Ka Alitjinya pakanu, munu watjanu, "Nya:kuna nyuranya kulini? Nyalpi alatjitu nyura!"

Ka alatji watjanyangka Nyalpi uwankara pakara pintjantjararingkula parpakanu Alitjila, ka mi:na kutjara katuringkula, ngulu mirangu munu wankaringu. Munu nyangu palumpa kangkuru milpatjunkunyangka. Ka watjanu, "Pakala malany, mungaringanyi nyanga," munu paluru nyalpi tjuta mantjinu Alitjinya yu:npa nguru. Panya punkanu nyalpi tjuta punu itara nguru, munuya Alitjila mulyangka ngaringi.

Ka Alitjinya pakara watjanu, "Awari tjukurmanangina, kutjupa kutjupa." Munu uwankara tjakultjunangi kangkurungka.

"Be quiet!" roared the Witch.

"I won't!" shouted Alitji.

"Off with her head!" shouted the Witch, her face crimson with fury.

Nobody moved.

"What am I listening to you for?" Alitji demanded. "Why—you're all just a lot of leaves, anyway!"

As she said this, the whole lot of them turned into bats and came flapping down towards her. She raised her hands and tried to ward them off, giving a little scream, half in fear, half in anger—and then she awoke.

There was her sister, still crooning to herself as she played milpatjunanyi and told her stories.

"Wake up, little sister," she said to Alitji as she gently brushed away some fallen leaves that had fluttered down from the river gum upon Alitji's face. "It's getting late."

"Oh, I've had such a strange dream!" Alitji said. And she began to tell her sister all the strange adventures she had been dreaming about.

Alitji woke up to find it had all been a strange dream.

Ka Alitjinya wankaringu munu watjanu, "Awari! Tjukurmanangina kutjupa kutjupa".

GLOSSARY

Ainkura (puffball) is a sort of inedible toadstool.

Ant-lions are large ants which dig a deep-sided pit into sandy soil.

The **Bandicoot** is a small, insectivorous and herbivorous Australian marsupial. It looks a little like a very large rat.

A **Billy (can)** is a container for the boiling of water or the making of tea, over an open fire. It is usually made from tin with a wire handle. Hence 'billy tea' is made in a billy-can.

Bush is uncultivated Australian woodland.

Cassia is a flowering shrub.

A **claypan** is a shallow depression in clayey soil, that fills with water after rain.

Corkwood is the common name given to an Australian tree with coarse cork-like bark. It bears yellow flowers rich in nectar which Aboriginal people use to sweeten drinks.

A **cooroboree** is an Aboriginal sacred or festive gathering with songs and dance.

Damper is a large scone loaf baked in the ashes of a fire.

A **digging stick** is like a crowbar made of wood, scraped smooth, pointed at one end and hardened in the fire. It is used for digging such foods as honey ants, root vegetables and goanna eggs from hard ground.

A **dilly bag** is a small, knotted-string carry bag.

Honey ants – sometimes called 'honey-pot ants' – are a type of ant able to store a honey-like liquid in their distended crop.

An **initiate** is a young man who has recently been through the rites that enable him to take his place in the tribe as an adult.

Itunypa is a root vegetable that has an extremely strong flavour.

Mulga is a type of tree found in the drier parts of Australia. Also refers to the bush, the back country.

Ochre is red- or yellow-coloured clay.

Perenti is the largest Australian lizard, dark in colour with large, pale yellow spots.

Quandongs are small, bright red, globular drupes; their taste is similar to that of guavas.

A **river gum** is a type of very large eucalyptus tree, found along water courses in the drier parts of Australia.

Spinifex is a coarse grass with spiny leaves that grow in large clumps over much of inland Australia.

A **stockman** is a man employed to tend livestock, especially cattle.

Tea-tree is a flowering shrub.

Tecoma is the large shrub from whose bamboo-like branches the shafts of hunting spears are made.

Tinka – a small lizard.

Tjintjulu are shiny, bright, inedible berries, about the size of a pea. Aboriginal girls twine strands of hair around tiny sticks and then push them into the tjintjulu. This is a very decorative way of dressing hair.

Wild tomato is the common name given to the fruit of a small, purple-flowering plant. It belongs to the same family as the potato.

Witchety grubs are the fat, creamy-brown coloured larvae of certain beetles, found in the branches and roots of some types of trees and shrubs. They are nutritious, salty-flavoured and considered a great delicacy.

A **woomera** (throwing stick) is the wooden implement into which spears are fitted for throwing.

A **wurlie** is a shelter made of branches and bark, and thatched with leaves or spinifex grass.

Yam is a starchy, tuberous root vegetable.

NOTES TO *ALITJI*

This edition of *Alice in Wonderland* marks the 125th anniversary of the first publication of Lewis Carroll's famous tale. The Reverend Charles Lutwidge Dodgson, using the pseudonym Lewis Carroll, wrote the first version of his story, which he called *Alice's Adventures under Ground*, in 1862-3. This was a handwritten manuscript which he illustrated himself. The first published edition of *Alice's Adventures in Wonderland* – Carroll's new title for his story – with illustrations by Sir John Tenniel, was printed by the Clarendon Press at Oxford and issued by Macmillan in London in 1865. This was a rewritten, expanded version of the original manuscript. By 1884, one edition after another had been sold out, and a total of 100 000 copies produced. Following Dodgson's death in 1898, copyright in *Alice* expired in 1907. Since that date, the story has been produced in many forms in the English language, its text often altered and adapted, and it has been illustrated by many different artists. There have been nursery editions, miniature editions, *de luxe* editions, comic-strip versions; the story has been adapted for plays, it has been filmed, broadcast, televised and recorded, and its verse has been set to music. Through everyday objects such as crossword- and jigsaw-puzzles, games, toys, biscuit-tins, china and nursery furniture. Alice and her Wonderland have become familiar as household words, while legions of little girls have worn blue dresses, frilled pinafores and striped stockings at innumerable fancy-dress parties.

These first translations of *Alice* – into French and German – were published in 1869, soon to be followed by editions translated and produced by Swedish, Italian, Danish, Dutch and Russian publishers. A total of forty-three foreign-language translations of *Alice* have in fact been published, often in many different editions. These include Arabic, Chinese, Finnish, Greek, Hebrew, Icelandic, a number of Indian languages, Japanese and Swahili, besides other African languages. In addition, Braille, Esperanto, Pidgin and Shorthand editions have been published. A checklist of the different translations and their editions may be found in Warren Weaver's fascinating book *Alice In Many Tongues* (The University of Wisconsin Press, Madison, 1964).

In 1974 *Alitjinya Ngura Tjukurtjarangka*, the Pitjantjatjara version of *Alice*, became, the forty-fourth translation of the story into another language. Pitjantjatjara is the language of the Pitjantjatjara people, who inhabit South Australia and the Northern Territory. It is only in recent years that the Pitjantjatjara language was given a written form. Nancy Sheppard, who has adapted and translated this Pitjantjatjara version, has been very active in producing texts and tapes for the intensive course in the language offered by Adelaide University. For nine years, Ms Sheppard taught Pitjantjatjara children at Ernabella, near Alice Springs. She produced this version of the story with Aboriginal children very much in mind, and her manuscript has evoked a delighted response from those with whom she has shared the story.

Like all languages, Pitjantjatjara is the cultural expression of its people, descriptive of the terrain, the fauna and flora and the way of life known to them; it follows that the characters and setting of *Alice* have been adapted accordingly. The White Rabbit, with his gloves and fan, becomes the Kangaroo, with dilly-bag and digging-stick – not, it should be emphasized, because there is no Pitjantjatjara word for 'rabbit', but simply because an Aboriginal Alice would naturally have seen a kangaroo in her dream. The Caterpillar becomes a Witchety Grub; the pepper in Lewis Carroll's chapter titled *Pig and Pepper* becomes *itunypa* root, while the baby in that chapter changes, not into a pig, but into a native bandicoot. The prickly Australian echidna replaces the hedgehog at the Queen's croquet party, which, in this version, becomes the Game of the Witch Spirit; and the invitation from the Queen (the Witch Spirit) to the Duchess (the Spirit of the North Wind) is sent by smoke-signal. Possibly the most interesting aspect of the whole project, however, is not the devising of ingenious substitutions to fit cultural demands, but the fact that the Pitjantjatjara version succeeds as a story to be appreciated and enjoyed, chuckled over and remembered, demonstrating (for the forty-fourth time) in a language other than English, the universality of Lewis Carroll's imagination.

Lewis Carroll's original story is, of course, appreciated on one important level for its subtlety of language, its exercises in logic (and illogic), plays upon words, and verse parodies. Even in these respects, Nancy Sheppard's translation is often remarkably true to the original. She has succeeded in introducing into her Pitjantjatjara version and its English translation a number of puns. In Chapter Seven, for example, she has followed Carroll in introducing a good deal of word-play in the Koala's (otherwise the Dormouse's) story. '"In a far country," (the Koala began) "there were three little girls, all sisters, called Tili, Iltji and Itjila. All three lived in a tank."'

This compares with Carroll's: '"Once upon a time there were three little sisters," the Dormouse began in a great hurry; "and their names were Elsie, Lacie, and Tillie; and they lived at the bottom of a well–".' *Tili*, in Pitjantjatjara, means 'flame', 'firestick' or 'match'; *Iltji*, besides being the Pitjantjatjara translation of 'Elsie', also means 'wilderness' or 'desert'; and *Itjila* is an anagram of 'Alitji' (just as Carroll's 'Lacie' is an anagram of 'Alice'). All three Pitjantjatjara words are acceptable names. The word *tangka* means both 'tank' and 'cooked food'.

With this knowledge, the puns become clear in their context:

> '"What did they live on?" Alitji asked.
>
> '"Cooked food," said the Koala.
>
> 'Much surprised, Alitji said, "But how could they cook it?"
>
> '"On a fire, of course," said the Koala. "Don't forget they had Tili."'

In Carroll's original text, the well in which the three sisters live is, it transpires, a treacle well (based, it is thought, on a 'treacle well' near Oxford – 'treacle' being an old term given to medicinal compounds: a treacle well was one which contained water believed to be of medicinal value.) The Dormouse continues:

> '". . . And so these three little sisters – they were learning to draw, you know–"
>
> '"What did they draw?" said Alice, quite forgetting her promise.
>
> '"Treacle," said the Dormouse . . .'

Much of the 'logical nonsense' dialogue has been translated, too; and Pitjantjatjara children know many songs, some of which have been adapted for the Pitjantjatjara version, while in the English (or Australian) translation of the Pitjantjatjara, there is for example, a parody of *Waltzing Matilda*.

This Australian edition of *Alice*, in the manner of one of the Chinese and one of the Japanese editions, gives an English translation alongside the Pitjantjatjara text.

The first edition of *Alitji* was illustrated by Byron Sewell, an avid collector of Lewis Carroll's works. Sewell, who was deeply impressed by Aboriginal art, showed me some pictures for *Alice* which he had based on Aboriginal x-ray technique and suggested these might be used to illustrate an Australian edition in the English language. (This incidentally, would have been the first English language edition ever produced in Australia, since every other edition had been imported.) I thought it would be more innovative and exciting to produce an Aboriginal language version to accompany Sewell's illustrations – and so the original collaboration between illustrator, editor and translator began. In retrospect, it seems inappropriate to have used artwork by a non-Aboriginal to illustrate the Pitjantjatjara text. For this second edition of *Alitji*, Donna Leslie has created new illustrations which give the story a new and glowing perspective.

The decision of Mr J. W. Warburton, then Director of the Department of Adult Education at Adelaide University, to support the project by publishing an educational edition in 1975, and the subsequent allocation of funds for this purpose by the Federal Department of Aboriginal Affairs were warmly welcomed.

The chief aim of artist, translator and editor was to present this timeless and universal story to the Aboriginal child, and at the same time, through the English translation of the Pitjantjatjara version, to acquaint other children – and adults – with some knowledge of Aboriginal culture.

Here, then, is the second edition of the forty-fourth version of *Alice in Wonderland* in another tongue; that of a people whom Alice Liddell, the little girl for whom Lewis Carroll wrote his story, might have described, from the far distance of her English home in Oxford, as 'upside-down'. And here, to end this introduction to *Alitji* in Lewis Carroll's words, is a final quotation from the original English text as Alice falls down the rabbit hole:

'"I wonder if I shall fall right *through* the earth! How funny it'll seem to come out among the people that walk with their heads downwards! The Antipathies, I think–" (she was rather glad there *was* no one listening, this time, as it didn't sound at all the right word) "–but I shall have to ask them what the name of the country is, you know. Please, Ma'am, is this New Zealand or Australia?" (and she tried to curtsey as she spoke – fancy *curtseying* as you're falling through the air! Do you think you could manage it?) "And what an ignorant little girl she'll think me for asking! No, it'll never do to ask: perhaps I shall see it written up somewhere."'

Barbara Ker Wilson

Point Halloran, Queensland, 1991

ABOUT THE PITJANTJATJARA LANGUAGE

Pitjantjatjara, one of the Western Desert group of languages, is widely spoken in the west of South Australia and across its borders into Western Australia and the Northern Territory. It is expressive of the rich ancient culture of the people of the Musgrave and Mann Ranges, and is gentle to the ear. In some South Australian schools Pitjantjatjara is taught as the first language, and in some schools and tertiary institutions as a second language.

It will be helpful for speakers of English wanting to read the Pitjantjatjara version to know that the consonants are pronounced more or less as they are in English and that *a* is pronounced as in *pass*, but a bit shorter; *i* as in *hill*, and *u* as in *put*. Stress falls on the first syllable of each word, so then Alitji is pronounced *A'litji.*

ACKNOWLEDGEMENT

I am grateful to Yanyi Baker for her interest in the creation of *Alitji*, and for her pertinent criticism of the completed text.